A Fateful Fall

When Ruby saw the rider fall, she ran to his side. He was lean and elegant.... His eyes were gray. In one tiny fraction of time Ruby's world had turned upside down, and she knew why.

She had only played at being in love before; this was the real thing.... She wanted to rest her hand against his cheek and tell him of her feelings. She yearned to lean forward and touch his mouth with her own, even though she had only that second encountered him...

The earl looked at his rescuer. Her hair was like black satin, her eyes dark brown and luminous.... Her nearness was the most potent aphrodisiac he had ever known.

"You are the beginning of my life," he said very softly. "I will love you from this moment on until my ending."

THE REGENCY JEWEL SERIES
by Helen Ashfield
published by St. Martin's Press

EMERALD

SAPPHIRE

PEARL

GARNET

RUBY

OPAL*

*forthcoming

Ruby

Helen Ashfield

ST. MARTIN'S PRESS/NEW YORK

St. Martin's Press titles are available at quantity discounts for sales promotions, premiums or fund raising. Special books or book excerpts can also be created to fit specific needs. For information write to special sales manager, St. Martin's Press, 175 Fifth Avenue, New York, N.Y. 10010.

RUBY

Copyright © 1984 by Pamela Bennetts

All rights reserved. No part of this book may be used or reproduced in any manner whatsoever without written permission except in the case of brief quotations embodied in critical articles or reviews. For information address St. Martin's Press, 175 Fifth Avenue, New York, N.Y. 10010.

Library of Congress Catalog Card Number: 84-13027

ISBN: 0-312-90318-9

Printed in the United States of America

First St. Martin's Press mass market edition/March 1987

10 9 8 7 6 5 4 3 2 1

Acknowledgements

To the following authors I offer my most grateful thanks. Without their scholarship and fascinating books I would not have been able to write this novel:

Human Documents of Adam Smith's Time, E. Royston Pike.
Human Documents of the Industrial Revolution, E. Royston Pike.
The Making of the Machine Age, Jacynth Hope-Simpson.
Fabrics and Clothing, J.M. Holt.
The Skilled Labourer. J.L. Hammond & Barbara Hammond.
The Industrial Revolution in the 18C, Paul Mantoux.
Factory Life and Work, Frank E. Huggett.
How They Lived, Asa Briggs.
Clothing: The Essentials of Life Series, Lt. Col. F.S. Brereton.
A History of Everyday Things in England 1733-1851, Majorie & C.H.B. Quennell.
The Craftsman in Textile, Leslie J. Clarke.
Portrait of Lancashire, Jessica Lofthouse.
Lancashire Villages, Jessica Lofthouse.
A History of Lancashire, J.H. Bagley.
Handbook of English Costume in the 18C, C. Willett Cunnington and Phillis Cunnington.
Dress and Undress, Iris Brooke.
The Eighteenth Century. Costume Reference 4, Marion Sichel.
Dress in Eighteenth Century England, Anne Buck.
Occupational Costume in England, Phillis Cunnington and Catherine Lucas
Costume and Fashion 1760-1920, Jack Cassin-Scott.
A Woman's Place, Majorie Filbee.
Domestic Life in England, Norah Lofts.

One

Lancashire 1790

The kitchen was filled with sunlight and the smell of hot bread. The loaves were golden-brown and crusty, begging to be cut into thick slices and spread with freshly-churned butter and plum jam.

Ruby Travers, just turned sixteen, loved baking days. They were what she called one of her 'red days' and she was always ready to help Mrs. Sugarwhite, the cook, to prepare the brick oven beside the huge fireplace. Bundles of faggots first, then hot ashes to ignite them. When she was a child she had hopped impatiently from foot to the other, waiting for the sticks to burn to ashes. Cook had said she was as wick as a snig, her Lancashire way of telling Ruby she was a fidget.

Ruby had learned soon enough that one couldn't hurry an oven, biding her time until she could fill the cavern with pies, bread and, if it were a special occasion, a rich pound cake.

She had grown tidier too. She no longer had to be reminded to sweep the hearth until it was clean enough to eat from. She applied plenty of elbow grease to the seats on each side with little cupboards under them. One contained some baccy, a treat for old Ruer who came now and then to labour in the overgrown garden. The other concealed a bottle of rum from which Sally Sugarwhite took a nip when she was 'thronged', or unduly busy.

'Grey days' included those on which the laundry had to be tackled. Once a month all the dirty linen and clothes were gathered together in great heaps. Lizzie Farnworth would come up from the village, glad to earn sixpence a day plus breakfast and dinner. Then the outhouse would be filled with steam and the smell of strong soap. Everyone would get red hands and aching backs, their tempers worn thin by evening.

Ruby turned from the window, filled with utter contentment as she looked about her. Waterfields was the only home she had ever known. When she was only a few weeks old her mother, Vinnie, had come there to be Sir Warren Askwith's housekeeper. She had grown up in the small but exquisite Elizabethan house not far from the village of Cocker Booth and in the shadow of Pendle Hill.

Every inch of it was precious to her, from the panelled hall to the tiny attic where she had her truckle bed. She pretended it belonged to her as she polished floors and furniture or ran an affectionate hand along the banister rail which time had worn to the smoothness of satin.

Warren Askwith was as poor as a church mouse. Many of Waterfields' treasures had had to be sold to pay for the necessities of life. It made Ruby sad when a painting or a piece of silver had to go, for they were like old friends. She didn't blame Askwith. He didn't gamble or drink or keep loose women. Indeed, he seemed innocent of any vice, spending his days reading in his library or walking on the moors. He had inherited crippling debts from his father and, by nature, was totally unfitted to cope with the burdens and complexities of living.

The staff wasn't really large enough to run the place, but it was all he could afford. Apart from Vinnie and cook there was just Elsie Ramsbottom, who was both scullery and dairymaid, and Ruby herself who turned her hand to anything which needed to be done.

Until six months ago Mrs. Boddy had been there as well, doing a bit of sewing or rubbing up cutlery and what ornaments were left. She had been Askwith's nurse, but had grown too old to be useful and had gone to live with her married daughter. Everyone below stairs had wept as they said goodbye to her, but they understood there wasn't the money to maintain idle hands. Nanny Boddy had been a part of Waterfields and to Ruby it was like the loss of yet another treasure.

Ruby loved the surrounding countryside almost as much as she cared for the house itself. Cocker Booth had its heels dug defiantly into a steep hillside. The gritstone cottages huddled together as if to protect each other from the harsh elements. But Waterfields lay in a slight dip in the land, proud and serene, too sure of itself to bother about bad weather.

When Ruby was young she thought Pendle Hill was the biggest mountain on earth, despite the fact that it was less than two thousand feet above sea-level. It shewed a bleak face to Pendle Forest, but on the opposite flank it was gentler, smiling down on the hamlets and villages below its summit.

It was witch country and there were many who still believed in the power of the women who had terrified folk in the seventeenth century and had paid the ultimate price for it. Ruby didn't believe in witches and had no patience with such dark memories.

She found her pleasures in the high, rolling moors which seemed to have no end and in the fast-running streams which sparkled like diamonds melted by the sun. She knew every oak tree, whitethorn and beech for ten miles around as she walked across field and farmland, hearing the comforting sound of sheep and the call of the curlew. All her life she had dwelt amongst green pastures, small woods, twisting tracks which climbed heavenwards, and cloughs, or valleys, which made deep slashes in the landscape. It was her world and she never wanted to leave it.

Her favourite walk was to Trawley Dale, a derelict village not far from Roughlee. The cottages there had no roofs, and doors hung by a single hinge. The grass was knee-high and stumps of trees were covered with moss and lichen as Nature took back what she had once given to its former inhabitants. It was here that Ruby pretended she met the man she was going to marry. She knew exactly what he looked like, for she had thought about it a great deal. He would be strong and well-built, with fair hair, a wide smile and a voice filled with love and humour. She wasn't quite sure what he should be wearing, for Askwith was no guide to fashion. The *beau-monde* never came near Waterfields and the farmers and their hands wore smocks, loose breeches and mud-caked boots. It was a minor detail and it didn't spoil the dream at all.

She came out of her reverie as her mother called her to table. Sally had made griddle cakes on a flat iron dish over the fire, and there was the promised bread and preserve, with hot, sweet tea to wash it down.

Ruby glanced round at her companions and smiled. Vinnie was thirty-eight, on her own since her daughter's birth. She was a gentle, patient woman with light brown hair, hazel eyes and a mouth which hinted of some inner sadness. She was a hard worker, but had always got a moment or two to listen to Ruby's tales of what she had seen or done on any particular day. She was there to bathe a cut knee and to kiss tears away when they were shed.

Vinnie never spoke about Ruby's father. Ruby had often asked questions about him but they were turned aside or left unanswered. After a while she stopped enquiring about him. It seemed to upset her mother and she thought perhaps he might have been a ne'er-do-well whose existence was best forgotten now he was in his grave.

Cook was stout with ruddy cheeks and eyes like periwinkles. She was a good-tempered soul, except on wash-days, and she had a great fondness for the housekeeper's daughter whom she thought a right gradely lass.

Elsie Ramsbottom was fourteen, thin as a bean-pole, with an insatiable appetite and a tongue which was never still. Sally said darkly that she was better to follow than to face, for the scullerymaid was somewhat homely. Still, as cook admitted somewhat grudgingly, she was energetic and never had the sulks, and that was something in her favour.

"Mother." Ruby reached for another griddle cake, delicious as the pat of butter melted into it. "Elsie says I look just like the portrait of Lady Helen Askwith. You know, the one the carter came to fetch the other day. I do hope I am, for she was so lovely."

Vinnie raised her head and for a second Ruby saw something in her mother's eyes which startled her.

"You're not in the least like her, and not so much conceit if you please. As for you Elsie Ramsbottom, you should have something better to do than moon over old pictures and put silly ideas into other people's heads."

It was wholly out of character for Mrs. Travers to be so sharp and they all stared at her in astonishment. Ruby coloured uncomfortably, feeling quite put down and unsettled by the extraordinary change in her mother.

"I'm sorry. I didn't mean to be vain."

"No, no, I'm the one to be sorry." Vinnie's flash of temper was over and she was contrite. "I'm a grump to-day. Don't pay me any heed."

"Have you got another headache?" Vinnie often had headaches and it bothered Ruby. "Shall I get you some of that medicine which Dr. Hornby gave you?"

"No, dear, it's nothing. I'll have another cup of tea instead. Do me more good than potions and pills."

"That's what I always say." Sally picked up the tea-pot and began to fill Vinnie's cup. "Plenty of cures to be found in the hedgerows without turning to the muck made up by gaumless fooils what don't know what they're doing."

Ruby hesitated. In the light of Vinnie's sudden outburst this wasn't the ideal time to raise a matter she had been keeping to herself since that morning. However, if she left it much longer it might seem that she was being secretive. Besides, she was bursting to tell everyone the news.

"Mother."

"Yes, love?"

"I haven't had the chance to mention this yet, seeing we've been so busy, but Sir Warren has given me a present."

"Oh?"

Vinnie was wary and Ruby's heart sank as she watched the cup shake in her mother's hand. It hadn't been the right time, and she should have left it until they were alone. But it was too late now for regrets and she went on rapidly, wanting to get it over.

"Yes, it's a dress. He said he was sorry he forgot my birthday last week, but when he went to Blackburn he saw it in a shop. It's dark red, with the fullest skirt imaginable and very tight sleeves. The neck's rather low, but there's a sort of scarf to tuck into the bodice. Sir Warren said it's a buffon. Shall I go and get it?"

It seemed an eternity before Vinnie spoke and when she did her voice was tight and controlled as if she were trying to hold back some fierce emotion.

"I can't think for the life of me why he should do such a thing. He's never given you anything before."

"No, but it was my birthday and …"

Ruby's words trailed away in the cloud of her mother's displeasure.

"Maybe so, but you've had other birthdays he's paid no heed to. What's more, there's no call for him to go wasting what little he's got on such fripperies. We need money for food, the roof wants repairing, and Elsie and Mrs. Sugarwhite haven't had any wages for two months. He'd no right to be so prodigal."

"Don't moither yourself, m'dear." Sally was frowning. She'd never seen Vinnie in such a state. Everyone else had ups and downs but never Mrs. Travers, that is, not until now. It wasn't such a dreadful thing after all and, wages or no wages, she thought it was a reet kindly gesture the master had made. "Elsie and me can manage a bit longer. We've got enough to eat and a bed to sleep in, which is more than many folk can say. Let t' lass put it on. Cheer us all up."

Ruby could see the refusal on Vinnie's lips, as perplexed as Mrs. Sugarwhite. The headache must be worse than usual but at last she got a reluctant nod of agreement.

As she went upstairs Ruby pondered on her mother's strange behaviour. She knew it wasn't because Vinnie didn't like Sir Warren. He had always shewn her mother the greatest respect, as if she were a lady and not his housekeeper at all. He smiled at her in his sweet, almost boyish manner, even holding doors open for her and giving her a funny little bow when he walked away.

As for Vinnie, she fussed over the master as if he were a duke, always insisting that everything should be done properly as it had been in the old days before the family had lost its fortune. "He's a real gentleman," she would say. "Not like some who pretend to be what they aren't. His blood is blue, and don't you forget it."

But then Ruby's concern melted away as she took the gown from the clothes-chest. It was pure silk, shimmering in the light, and exactly what she would have chosen herself for a meeting with her imaginary loved-one in Trawley Dale.

She wasn't sure whether she'd got the buffon arranged correctly, but at least it made her decent, and she ran downstairs to seek approbation.

Sally's and Elsie's reaction left nothing to be desired. Both cried out in amazement at the transformation, telling Ruby she looked every inch a lady and the prettiest thing one could hope to meet.

Ruby gave Vinnie a swift look, hoping for acceptance if not praise, but when her mother spoke all the joy went out of the moment.

"Please go and take if off," said Vinnie quietly but very firmly. "It isn't at all suitable for you and I shall ask Sir Warren to return it to the shop. It's not seemly that he should spend so much on you, and you'll have no occasion to wear such a thing in this house."

"But, mother ..."

"Do as I ask." Vinnie's lips were compressed and Ruby

could see there was no hope of her relenting. "I'll speak to the master about it to-night. If there's a shilling or two left over at the end of the quarter I'll think about getting a few yards of printed cotton. That will be much more suitable for your station in life."

Ruby said nothing more. She removed the offending garment and then went to Vinnie's room to lay it across the coverlet. She didn't cry, although she felt very much like doing so. She was sixteen now and grown up people didn't grizzle over a dress. In a way she could see Vinnie's point of view. She could hardly wear her beautiful present when she was doing her chores or scrambling up steep hills. She was also beginning to feel guilty about the wages owed to cook and Elsie. They'd had to go without what they'd worked so hard for, simply because Sir Warren hadn't stopped to think what he was doing.

But she couldn't rid herself of the notion that there was more to her mother's totally unexpected tartness than the fact that Askwith had squandered a few guineas he couldn't afford. She sensed it went much deeper than that. She had no idea what was wrong, but she knew she couldn't ask her mother to explain. It was something private and important and not for her to know.

"Oh, Gervase," she said aloud, for so she had named her imaginary hero. "I'm sorry you won't see me in it after all, but we can pretend I've got it on, can't we? I can wear pearls and have a fan made of ivory and ostrich feathers. I can do anything I like in Trawley Dale, even if I'm only a servant here."

She smoothed her hair, put on her old fustian dress and white apron and went back to the kitchen. Her mother didn't look at her, but cook and Elsie gave her sympathetic grins.

She returned their smiles and made her way to the sink to peel the potatoes for supper. She knew Vinnie wouldn't mention the subject again and neither would she.

She had been a grand lady for just three minutes. Now she

was a maid again and likely to remain one for a very long time to come.

* * *

The next day Mr. Lionel Whitcome, the owner of two cotton mills in the area, paid a visit to Waterfields. He called at least once every three weeks and everyone dreaded the sight of his sturdy, well-clad figure striding up to the front door.

He lived in a house at Stonebanks, but it wasn't an old one like Askwith's. It had been built some twenty years before and, as Vinnie often said, was as jumped up as its owner.

Whitcombe's blood, unlike Askwith's, was far from blue. He was one of the new capitalists who, in addition to his factories in Lancashire and Derbyshire, had accumulated great wealth by shipping cotton, sugar and human beings from one part of the globe to another. His coffers were full, his wardrobe vast. Every stick of furniture had cost enough to keep a poor family for a year, but still he hadn't been satisfied. There had been something lacking, but he didn't know what it was until one day when he rode past Waterfields.

He knew immediately that it was what he had been searching for. It wasn't just a question of four walls and a roof. It was a way of life which he had never been able to attain in spite of his fortune. It became an itch, a burr and an obsession and, once he had made up his mind to have it, he gave Warren no peace.

At first he'd tried to ingratiate himself with his neighbour. He knew Askwith was near to ruin and felt confident the latter would jump at the chance of selling for a fair price. But, like many weak and indecisive men, Warren could be stubborn when he chose, and he was quite intractable about Whitcombe's proposal.

He had looked at the merchant as if he'd been scum and Whitcombe had felt his choler rise. A near-begger, yet the man had the arrogance of a kind, and his terse words had struck home. It had infuriated Whitcombe and made him all the more determined to get his own way.

Each time he called there were arguments. The servants listened to the raised voices coming from the library. Whitcombe's were rough and harsh; Warren's high-pitched and near to breaking-point.

Whenever Askwith had to sell something, Lionel always seemed to find out about it, paying the agent over the odds, and fulsome in his praise of the object in question when he next encountered Sir Warren.

It was Ruby who led Whitcome to the library that day. She hated him most heartily for what he was trying to do, for it was as if he were stealing something from her. It hurt her, too, to see Sir Warren so upset and her eyes smouldered as she stood back to let Whitcombe enter the room.

When the shouting began Elsie ran to the library door to listen, as she always did. She crouched down by the key-hole so that she shouldn't miss a word. After a while she crept away, her face drained of colour, and went to report to Mrs. Travers and cook who were waiting apprehensively in the kitchen.

"Well?" Mrs. Sugarwhite was impatient. "Did you hear owt? What's going on i' there?"

"They're fratching worse than ever." Elsie's voice wasn't quite steady. "Never heard the likes of it before."

"Go on, what are they saying?"

"You're as white as a sheet, Elsie," said Ruby, coming forward to take the maid's cold hand. "Are you all right? You needn't worry, you know. He won't hurt you."

"Maybe not me but someone here's going to get hurt. He was on again about buying the house. Sir Warren said his forebears had walked with princes while Mr. Whitcombe's were grovelling i' t' dirt like serfs. That did it, I can tell you. Frightened the wits out of me when Mr. Whitcombe started to bawl. I thought t' door were going to burst open."

"But what did he say?"

"He said he'd never forgive master for that, and he'd make him eat his words before he was done."

"Oh dear." Vinnie was pale as well, her clenched hands betraying her anxiety. "I do hope there's not going to be real trouble. Why does the wretched creature keep coming here to plague Sir Warren?"

"'Cos he knows master's got no money." Elsie was very down to earth and recovering from her fright now that she was back with her friends. "Those what haven't got money can't fight as hard as those what have. I know one of Mr. Whitcombe's girls; we goes to chapel together sometimes. She says it's well-known he never forgives an insult and those who have rubbed him up the wrong way always pay i' t' end."

"It's so unfair." Ruby was hot with indignation. "How dare he push in here and bellow like a street vendor?"

"Reckon that's just what he is." Cook was disparaging. "No better than a pedlar when all's said and done. Not a drop of breeding in him, but Elsie's right. I've heard that he doesn't forget a slight."

"And that's not all." Elsie had got her second wind. "He said to master that one day he'd live here no matter what he had to do to get his way."

"What did Sir Warren say?" Vinnie was holding her breath. "The poor man; what did he say?"

"That he'd rather burn Waterfields to the ground than let Mr. Whitcombe poll ... poll ... I can't exactly remember t' word."

"Pollute," said Vinnie slowly. "He'd rather destroy what he loves so much than let Whitcombe pollute the place."

"Yes, that's it ... pollute." Elsie's eyes were like saucers. "You don't think he meant it, Mrs. Travers, do you? Master wouldn't really do that, surely?"

Vinnie didn't answer at once; then she saw that the others were looking to her for reassurance.

"No, no, of course he wouldn't. It's just a figure of speech. Ruby, that's the library bell. Go and shew that ...

that monster out, and let's pray he won't come back after this."

When Ruby closed the door behind the crimson-faced Whitcombe she leaned against it for a moment, closing her eyes and feeling the beauty and magic of Waterfields soothe and comfort her. She hoped Sir Warren would be able to hold out against the obnoxious merchant, not simply because she and her mother would be homeless if he didn't, but because Lionel Whitcombe had no business to be there.

Vinnie had said Sir Warren's threat was just a figure of speech, but Ruby didn't think so. She understood exactly what Askwith meant and, if Waterfields really had been hers, she would have said the same thing.

Rather than let Lionel Whitcombe take possession she would have got a tinderbox and razed the house to the ground. Waterfields would have understood. It would rather die with dignity in a cleansing fire than live on in shame and misery with such a master.

Sir Warren's ancestors hadn't built it for the likes of the merchant. It was a gentleman's abode, and Lionel Whitcombe didn't qualify.

* * *

There was a second caller that day. Cuddy Dalton was Vinnie's brother and, in Ruby's opinion, a complete wastrel. She disliked him almost as much as she did the merchant, because he sponged off her mother and was always whining that he couldn't get work no matter how he tried.

Vinnie had looked after him since he was a baby, for their parents had died of fever soon after his birth. Ruby thought her sense of responsibility towards him was almost unnatural, seeing Dalton was now a grown man. It was as if her mother were afraid of him, terrified in case he should suddenly turn violent and upset the tranquility of Sir Warren's home.

Before Ruby's birth, Vinnie had been in service in

Manchester. She had managed to get Cuddy a post as a stable-boy but that had meant hard work. He had soon run away, joining a band of gipsies and wandering about the countryside thieving and getting drunk. He still travelled with the Romanies and whenever they were near Cocker Booth, far too often for Ruby's liking, he would call on his sister and demand food, taking the last penny from her thin purse.

Ruby never made a secret of her contempt for her uncle. Vinnie was always pleading with her to be nice to him but Ruby flatly refused. She was a strong-spirited girl and her views were honest. She hated Cuddy and she didn't hide the fact. She let her eyes travel over him, slowly and dissectingly, until he bared his teeth.

"What you staring at?" he demanded shortly. "Got two heads, have I? Never dream I were your kin, way you treat me."

Vinnie rushed in to appease.

"We've had a bad day, Cuddy. Ruby didn't mean anything, did you dear? Get a plate for your uncle and give him a good helping of stew from the pot. You'll like it, Cuddy. Got a lot of meat in it as well as vegetables."

Ruby didn't move and Vinnie said imploringly:

"Ruby, didn't you hear me? Your uncle is hungry."

"He always is, but some have to work for their victuals."

"Please ... don't ..."

"You want to take a stick to that lass, Vin." Cuddy slumped in a chair by the table, sticking his elbows on it. "No manners and no sense of family."

"Family!" Ruby was scornful. "I don't think of you as family. As far as I'm concerned you're just a ..."

"Ruby!"

When she saw the tears in Vinnie's eyes, Ruby gave up. It was always the same and Cuddy had won as usual. Still, she'd made her point and she couldn't bear to see her mother cry. She had had to give in before, but never until she'd had her say. She wished she could stiffen Vinnie's backbone and make her see that her brother was nothing short of a criminal who lived with a bottle in one hand, but she knew she'd never succeed.

Cuddy leered at Ruby in triumph as she put the plate down in front of him. She watched in disgust as he gobbled up the food, even more sour when Vinnie furtively got her purse from under her apron and took out a coin or two.

"It's all I've got at the moment, Cuddy," said Vinnie apologetically. "I know it isn't much. I'm sorry."

"Why should you be?" demanded Ruby, her good intentions of keeping a still tongue in her head flying to the four winds. "If he wants money, let him go and earn it."

Cuddy pocketed the money without a word of thanks and turned to his sister.

"I've been reet poorly, Vin. Couldn't work, you see."

"You look healthy enough to me." Ruby made short work of the excuse. "More likely you've been at the bottle again."

"Oh, Ruby, please!"

Cuddy rose, ignoring his niece.

"It's all right, Vin. I'll make do with this for the moment. Be back some time next week. 'Spect you'll have a bit more for me then, don't you?"

When he had gone, Ruby said furiously:

"Mother, why do you give in to him like that? He's no good. He'd take your last farthing to buy gin, you know that. He's not ailing; he's a good-for-nothing. Why don't you tell him to keep away? Anyone would think you were frightened of him."

Vinnie gave a nervous laugh, but Ruby was still too cross to see the look in her eyes.

"I suppose I should, but after all he is my brother. My mother made me promise to look after him, and I brought him up as if he were my own child."

"He isn't a child now; he's twenty-eight and ought to know better. You're only ten years older than him."

"Don't go on about it, love, my head's aching again. And

please watch what you say when he's here. You'll really offend him one day with that blunt tongue of yours."

"I don't care if I do. He deserves it."

"But I care if I do. He deserves it."

Ruby put her arms round her mother and hugged her.

"All right, I'll be careful, but don't you go upsetting yourself about him. He's not worth it, even if you did bring him up. I'll make some tea; that always helps your headaches, doesn't it?"

They said no more, but as Ruby sipped her tea she was reflective. Perhaps one day Cuddy would quarrel with the gipsies he lived with. She's heard times enough how hot-tempered they were. Maybe they would fall out with her detested uncle and make away with him. Even the thought of it made her feel better, but it was a pity that Romanies couldn't deal with the merchant at the same time.

There was no gainsaying it. The world would be a very much better place without Lionel Whitcombe and the feckless Cuddy Dalton.

* * *

Two days later Ruby went to see Mrs. Albina Pittaway, a weaver who lived on the outskirts of Cocker Booth.

In the nine years that Ruby had been visiting the widow, learning how to weave best quality cotton and muslin, she had never seen the one-roomed cottage in a state of tidiness. Apart from the loom and stool, there was an array of baskets and barrels containing lengths of finished material. Brooms, clearly not used, were propped against the wall. Chickens perched noisily on the rafters from which hung Albina's drying petticoats and shifts. A welter of cooking pots and pans balanced precariously on a set of rickety shelves, and there was a mattress in one corner, blankets tossed hither and thither. On the opposite wall there was an incongruous touch of luxury in the shape of a large, gilt-framed mirror which Mrs. Pittiway had taken a fancy to on a trip to Bolton.

After the first six months of tuition, Ruby had been talking knowledgeably about heddles, laths, reeds and pulleys, as if she had been about the business for years. By the age of eight she had known how to fasten the warp to the two rollers, pulling it taut by means of a weight on the rear one and an attachment on the front. She could operate the pedals deftly, so that alternate warp threads rose and fell, forming the shed through which the shuttle was thrown with the weft thread.

She knew the history of John Kay's flying shuttle and how it had speeded up the process of weaving, allowing a single operator to increase the width of cloth. She was well-versed in later inventions, such as Richard Arkwright's water-frame, James Hargreaves's spinning jenny and Samuel Crompton's mule.

It was the latter, with its rollers and spindles, which produced for the first time a thread which was both strong and fine, enabling English weavers to make cotton and muslin as delicate as any which came from India or the East.

But, as Albina was always saying, times were changing. Although most weaving was still done in the cottages, spinning mills were springing up like mushrooms on the banks of fast-flowing streams which could turn the water-wheels powering new machinery.

Men and women no longer spun yarn in the old way, stopping when they felt like it to tend their gardens or live-stock, or gossip with their neighbours over a brew of beer.

They couldn't compete with the speed and efficiency of the factories, and there was great discontent and fear because their livelihoods were thus threatened. The mills drew labour like a magnet, not only from their immediate surroundings, but from towns and villages far away. The day of independence was over for the spinners; they were now simply cogs in a rapidly advancing textile industry from which there was no turning back.

It was Albina, a woman of some education, who had

persuaded Vinnie to let Ruby attend the local Dame School. Vinnie hadn't needed much prodding, for she wanted the best for her daughter, and was thankful that she was learning a good trade which would one day take her away from scrubbing and cleaning.

When Ruby had made the tea, her first task upon arriving at the cottage, Albina left the loom and went to sit by the fire.

"Well, and what's your news to-day?"

Ruby was unwrapping some Bath cakes, handing one to Mrs. Pittaway.

"Not much really. Cuddy came on Tuesday, begging as usual. I started to tell him what I thought of him but it upset mother so I had to stop. I wish he'd stay away, and Mr. Whitcombe as well."

Albina's bright black eyes turned to Ruby.

"Oh, so he's been calling again, has he? Same thing, I suppose? Wants to buy Waterfields."

"Yes, and there was a terrible scene. It made Elsie quite weak at the knees."

"Serves her right for listening at key-holes."

"Mm, but if she didn't we wouldn't know what was going on, would we?"

Mrs. Pittaway nodded, accepting the logic of Ruby's argument.

"Didn't make Sir Warren change his mind?"

"No, far from it. Elsie told us he said he's rather destroy the house than let Whitcombe have it. Why is he so hateful? He's very rich and he lacks for nothing. All Sir Warren has is Waterfields."

Albina gave a sardonic smile.

"He's got more than that, m'dear. He's got three hundred years of breeding behind him and that's what Lionel Whitcombe resents."

"Yes, that's what Sir Warren said, more or less. Elsie heard him say his forebears had walked with princes when Mr. Lionel's were still serfs."

"That'll have got him on the raw." Mrs. Pittaway took a large bite out of her cake and gave a snort of laughter. "Sir Warren'll have to watch his step. That common lump isn't the type to forgive a few home-truths."

Ruby felt a twitch of alarm.

"You don't think he'd do anything to the master, do you? I mean, he wouldn't hurt him or ...?"

"'Course he would, if he got the chance."

"That would be awful. I don't know what mother and I would do if things changed at Waterfields. She's been there so many years, and I couldn't bear to leave either. How would we earn our living?"

"Don't know about your mother, but you could keep yourself easily enough and her, too, come to that. Your weaving's as good as mine now."

"But I haven't got a loom or the money to buy yarn and bobbins and things like that."

"You will have, when I die."

"Die? You can't die! I won't let you."

Albina chuckled again, but more softly this time.

"You'll not be able to stop me, lass, when my hour comes. Miss me, will you?"

"You know I will." Ruby put her cup down and caught Mrs. Pittaway's hand. "If it wasn't for you I wouldn't have a trade, even if I can't carry it on yet. You've taught me everything and ... well ... I love you."

"Stuff and nonsense. Love me, indeed!" Mrs. Pittaway's words didn't match her tone. "Save your love for your man, whoever he's going to be. Meanwhile, don't you want to know what I meant about when I go?"

"Not really, because then I'd have to think about you not being here and I hate that."

"I'm not gone yet and stop being such a goose. I'm old, my pet, and my bones ache. Sometimes my heart aches, too, for I've never really got over losing Ben, even though he's been in his grave these last thirty years. You'll love like that; I can tell. Well, enough of that. When I die, I'm leaving you my loom, the stool, and all that goes with them. You'll get my three rings and a bit of money besides. Not much, mind. I haven't got all that to speak of, and too much would spoil that fiery will of yours. Money shouldn't be thrown in your lap. You'll be a better person if you have to work for it, mark my words."

Ruby was speechless. The thought of possessing the beautifully-wrought loom and polished shuttles stunned her. They were almost as important to her as Waterfields, but it had never occurred to her that one day they might be hers. She didn't pay much attention to the mention of rings. They probably were quite cheap ones, and there wouldn't be a lot of money either. Not that she wanted money from Albina, but the widow lived very simply in her shabby home and there was never much food about. Most days when she visited Mrs. Pittaway, Ruby brought with her a dish of custard or a few slices of meat. There wasn't a lot to spare, but Vinnie was as grateful to Mrs. Pittaway as Ruby was and always found something to tempt Albina's appetite.

"I don't know what to say." Ruby found her voice at last. "You've quite taken my breath away."

"Not for long, if I know you. I've watched you at the loom. You're a born weaver and you become part of it when you work the treadles. Taught a few wenches in my time, but never one as quick and cunning of hand as you."

"I think I'm going to cry."

"I'll throw you out if you do."

"But it's such a wonderful present, or rather it will be. But I hope I don't get it for years and years. I'd rather have you."

Albina ordered Ruby to the stool, pretending she wasn't wiping her eyes, grunting in faked displeasure when her apprentice gave her a smacking kiss on one withered cheek.

"Get along with you, and remember this when time comes for you to start on your own. Ha'pennies make pennies and pennies make pounds. You needn't worry about the pounds; they'll look after themselves."

"I'll remember, I promise. Oh thank you, dear Mrs. Pittaway, thank you. I'll keep the loom for as long as I live and I'll never forget you. I'll make my wedding gown on this when I find that man you were talking about."

"And you'll make a good job of it. I just wish I were going to be here to see you all dressed up, for you're a reet comely lass, and you'll look a treat. Yes, I'm sorry I'll miss that. If you stop that snivelling I'll tell you something."

Ruby gave her eyes a quick rub.

"I've stopped. What is it?"

The old lady smiled and bent down to pick up a straying shuttle.

"I think I love you, too, Ruby Travers. Aye, now I come to consider it I'm bluddy sure I do."

* * *

"Of course you may put the loom in the attic when the time comes." Warren Askwith had listened carefully to Ruby's excited words, smiling gently at the girl's rosy flush and dancing brown eyes. "There's the big room on the south corner; take that one."

"If you're sure ...?"

"I'm sure. This place is too big for one man. It should belong to a family, only I haven't got anyone now. Have I ever told you how splendid it was in the old days when we had parties and *bal masqués* and drums?"

Askwith had, but not only was Ruby very well-brought-up, but she never tired of hearing about Waterfields in its hey-day. She listened attentively, not missing a single detail, making responsive noises which brought happiness to Warren's eyes.

When he fell silent at last, Ruby could see the sadness in him. For some reason it reminded her of an incident which had taken place a week or two before. She had come upon Askwith and her mother on the landing of the first floor. They were a few feet apart, but neither moved nor spoke. It had seemed to Ruby that there was some kind of secret communication between them, but she had dismissed it as her imagination. Her mother had probably been asking Sir Warren what he wanted for his meal, and doubtless he had been as slow over deciding that as he was over everything else.

"I'm very grateful, truly I am." Ruby thought it was time she made a graceful exit, for Askwith would keep her standing there listening to reminiscences for hours if he got the chance. "I won't make any noise, and one day you'll be proud of my work."

He seemed to come back from a long way away, faint amusement touching his lips.

"Make all the noise you like, my dear. It will be better than the waiting silence I live with. As for being proud of you, I've no doubts about that either. I've seen some of the things you've made and your work is excellent, but that isn't the greatest gift God gave you, you know."

"Oh?" Ruby paused by the door, the cleaning out of the dairy forgotten for a moment. "What is then, sir?"

"You have many." Warren's voice was quiet, almost as if he were talking to himself. "Beauty and youth and compassion, but the most important of all is your stout heart. You're a fighter, Ruby; you always will be." He seemed to come out of his dream, his tone changing. "Dear God, I wish I'd been born like you. Oh how I wish I was a fighter like you."

TWO

Molly Caudle finished the last drop of weak tea and brushed a hand across her mouth.

She had been a doffer at Brindle Mill since she was eight. Now she was fourteen, but it felt to her as if she had already lived for a hundred years.

Her world comprised a stuffy area where large mules spun thousands and thousands of bobbins of cotton day after day after day. There was no ventilation to speak of; the atmosphere was hot and steamy; filaments of cotton filled the nose and throat to choking point. It was worse when it got dark. Then the candles were lit, their smoke adding to the stench.

She hurried back to the machines, ready to remove the full flyers and replace them with empty bobbins. If one of the men in charge saw any sign of slacking there would be a heavy price to pay.

Brindle Mill was a squat, four-storied building with fifty or so windows gazing over the valley in which it was situated. A fast-flowing stream came down from the hills surrounding it, powering its water-mill. On the high ground all about it were the cottages of the workers; gritstone and bleak, clinging to precipitous slopes as their inhabitants clung to life itself.

Molly and her two younger brothers, Fergus and Timothy, rose at four each morning. If there were any scraps of food going they shared them, giving most to two-year-old Gwen and four-year-old Beatie. Then they took the one lantern they possessed and tramped down the rough tracks to begin another day in hell.

When Molly got to the rollers her friend Daisy Froome was there, pretending to be busy.

"Molly, another lot came in to-day. Eighty of 'em, I heard tell, and one's simple. You know, like Tommy Gabb."

Molly did know. When the industrialists had run out of local labour they turned to other sources to keep their output up. The ideal answer had been found in the pauper children, looked after by parishes in London, Birmingham and other big cities. The parishes were glad to be rid of the responsibility of keeping their charges in the workhouses; the mill-owners were happy to take them. Some parishes drove hard bargains, insisting that one in twenty of their flock should be an idiot, for they all had their share of such unfortunates.

Hundreds of children arrived every week in Lancashire, Derby and other areas where the textile industry was booming. They were ideal for the purpose. Their fingers were small and nimble; they could get into nooks and crevices under the frames to pick up waste; they were easy to discipline, and their labour was ludicrously cheap.

"I pity 'em." Molly looked warily over her shoulder. Ham Walkden, her immediate overseer, had been watching her closely since first thing. She wasn't sure why, but she was taking no chances. "I've got to get back. Don't want no trouble."

"That Walkden's a pig; worst of the lot. Don't have to do owt to get a beating from him, but who's to know or care?"

Molly nodded. Daisy was right. The savage cruelty inflicted on the helpless children, paupers or otherwise, was kept within the mill walls. Society didn't want to know about ten-year-olds lashed with leather straps for failing to work fast enough, thus ensuring the foremen and overseers made their money. They weren't interested in the appalling accidents which occurred when tired limbs and eyes betrayed the young as they fell against moving parts of the machinery. They sat at their tables carving thick slices of roast beef, giving no thought to untold numbers of faces pinched with hunger and gaunt with fear. All they wanted was cheap and plentiful cotton.

"I'll make sure I keep out of his way. I must go, Daisy."

"I suppose we're lucky."

Molly stared at Daisy blankly.

"Lucky? Working here eighteen hours a day, bruises all over, and our bellies empty?"

"Well, we're not like them what come in the wagons, are we? We've got proper homes to go back to."

Molly's mouth twisted slightly.

She and her family lived in a cottage on the edge of Wellsand, the hamlet nearest to the mill. It was old, with holes in the roof and a floor which was never dry. There wasn't much furniture. One aged table which rocked when anything was put on it; three stools, a few pots and pans, and sacking serving as beds. Rats came out to look for crumbs but there were never any to be had. Every morsel of food was of crucial importance and had to be conserved.

Her mother, Mahala, had tuberculosis, growing frailer every day. She hadn't wanted her children to go to the mill, but there'd been no choice. The few pence they earned were just enough to keep actual starvation at bay, but she wept every night when she saw the state they were in. She bathed the angry red marks on their backs and put cold water on bruises turning purple and yellow. Each time she tended their wounds she demanded of God why it had to be like that, but she never got a reply.

"Yes, I suppose so." Molly brushed the thought of the cottage aside. It wasn't much of a home, but it was better than the apprentices' house run by the mill manager and his wife. Those who had the misfortune to be in their charge crept about as if they had all the cares of the world on their shoulders. "I really daresn't stop. If he sees me, you know what he'll do."

She collected the spools and went back to the frames,

wishing the day was at an end. She ached all over, her legs threatening to give way under her, and her stomach was desperate for a crust.

Then she heard Timothy scream, as she'd heard him do so many times before. Ham Walkden seemed to have a particular grudge against her brother and he was in a pitiable condition because of it.

"Stop it! Let him go, you spiteful beast."

Molly didn't know where the bravado came from which enabled her to grasp the overseer's arm and shout her fury at him.

At first, Walkden was so amazed that one of his victims should round on him in such a fashion that he simply stared at Molly. Then he kicked the sobbing Timothy out of his way and made for the girl who had dared to stand up to him.

Molly was vaguely aware of a circle of faces round her, mouths open, glazed eyes alert again for a moment or two. Reality was crowding in on her once more, her spurt of defiance gone as she backed away. She had long since got over the humiliation of being whipped in public. It happened to them all, over and over again.

To her vast surprise and infinite relief, Walkden didn't raise the strap he was carrying. Instead, he ordered the others back to their respective tasks, threatening dire consequences if another second was wasted.

Then he beckoned Molly to follow him to a small passage beyond the main room. It was colder there, bales stacked along the walls, dimly-lit.

She was shaking, terrified by the look he gave her, for she understood then why he had brought her there. Many of the older girls gave themselves willingly to their immediate masters in exchange for extra food or to escape punishment. No one had ever wanted Molly before, and even now she could hardly believe Walkden fancied her. He had a reputation as a womanizer, but his normal taste ran to females of buxom proportions who gave him his money's worth.

"Saucy madam, aren't you?" He looked her over thoughtfully. He hadn't noticed until the day before that under a covering of grime her hair was a wonderful reddish-gold and that her trembling lips were perfectly formed. Her blue eyes were fringed with dark lashes, dazzling in spite of her fear, and his loins were burning for her. "Know what you deserve, don't you?"

She remained mute, for his question was purely rhetorical.

"I could make it easy for you, of course." He was casual, not rushing things. "If you were to pleasure me for a while I might forget what you did just now."

Molly was transfixed. No words would come, for she had never expected to find herself in such a position, particularly with Walkden.

"Well, what's it to be? Haven't got all day. Going to oblige, are you, or shall I ..."

"No, no." Molly found her tongue at last, forced into a rapid decision. What she was going to do was wicked, and she knew it, but she hadn't healed from the last lot of stripes he'd given her. "I'll do what you say, but if I does ..."

He grinned almost benignly now that he'd got her agreement.

"Making terms are you? Aye, you're a sharp one, reet enough. What else do you want?"

"I want you to leave Timmy alone."

"The little tyke got what he asked for."

"He's had enough, Mr. Walkden. Couldn't really give me mind to pleasing you if I thought you were going to knock him about again."

He pursed his lips, torn between irritation and amusement. In the end he saw the funny side of it and there were plenty of other children to abuse.

"I'll leave him be for two days and that's my final offer."

It wasn't as much as Molly had hoped for, but it was better than nothing.

"All right; two days."

She shut her eyes as slowly and lasciviously he drew her threadbare dress down to her waist. Her breasts were only just starting to bud, but something about them made Ham sweat. He'd taken more women than he could count, but this one was different, stirring him to a fierce and inexplicable sexual desire.

At first he fondled her gently, not wanting his enjoyment to be over too soon. Then her soft, yielding flesh made his breath quicken and his grip tightened convulsively as his mouth sought hers.

His breath was fouler than all the smells of the mill mixed up together, but Molly hung on. Someone had to suffer and it was better that she did than Timmy. Perhaps if she could really satisfy Walkden she might win further reprieves for her brother. It was worth a try.

The floor pricked her with splinters, but she didn't notice them. She had had no experience of intercourse, but instinctively she knew what she had to do. She made herself relax, submitting to Ham's gross demands as if she were as aroused as he was. If she had cheated him, his wrath would fall on Timmy, not on her.

When it was over she got to her feet and pulled her dress up. She felt nothing. It was as if her body no longer belonged to her and she had no interest in what happened to it.

"You'll remember your promise?" she asked, watching Walkden fasten his belt. "You'll not touch Timmy?"

"Not for two days."

She knew he would keep his word. He was a savage, but he had his own self-made code of conduct to which he stuck rigidly. When her brother's period of safety was over perhaps she would smile at him in a certain way, or brush against him as she passed him by.

She walked back to the frame and the flyers, which needed to be changed again. Timmy was crouched by the rollers, waiting for her, his tear-stained face screwed up with guilt.

"I'm sorry, Moll," he said and caught her skirt. "I didn't mean to get you into trouble. Did he hurt you very much?"

She rested her hand on his head to comfort him.

"Weren't your fault, love, and he didn't hurt me at all."

She met the unspoken question in him with a brief smile.

"We came to an agreement, Mr. Walkden and me. He's promised not to touch you for two days. I'll try to get him to make it longer if I can. Don't fret, but you'd best be off now. Mustn't vex him again, must we?"

The boy hurried away, uncomprehending, but thankful for any respite.

Molly picked up the spools and held them tightly against her, just as she had held Ham Walkden. Nothing could change what had taken place and she might as well face that and make what use she could of her body. She had become like the rest of the girls, not a cut above them as she'd always imagined herself to be.

"Serves you right, Molly Caudle," she told herself silently. "Too stuck-up by half, that was your trouble. Now you're a whore like t'others."

Then her grief turned into audible words, drowned by the rattle and hum of the frames.

"I'm a bluddy trollop and I'll never be clean again. Oh, Jesus Christ, I wish I were dead."

* * *

Three months later October came in on flying wings. Clouds scudded across the sky; a nip in the air warned of winter's approach.

Ruby was returning from Roughlee and her phantom lover, almost within sight of Waterfields. She stopped to draw her hair up into its usual knot, pinning her plain, straw hat into position and smoothing her apron. Sir Warren's servants always had to look decent and tidy or face the rough side of Vinnie's tongue.

She was surprised when she saw the girl with the reddish-gold locks. Clearly she was a stranger, and there weren't many of those in the district. It was isolated and out of the way and few had reason to come there.

When Ruby got to within a few feet of the newcomer she stopped abruptly. She had never seen hair and skin so neglected before; the torn dress was no more than a rag. All paled into insignificance to Ruby as she stared in horror at the bruises and marks on the girl's arms and legs, and the look of utter defeat in her tired, blue eyes.

It wasn't a time to make polite conversation. It was an emergency and Ruby rose to the occasion. She had never had to deal with such a situation before, but she was armed with a kind and loving heart and a wealth of common-sense.

"I'm Ruby Travers," she said and smiled, although it was hard to do so in the face of such want and pain. "What's your name?"

At first she thought she would get no answer. The girl was hostile and also afraid. Finally she got a reply, bald and to the point.

"Molly Caudle, and I want a farthing to buy bread."

"You're hungry?"

"Yes, but the money's not for meself. It's to get a small loaf for my ma and brothers and sisters."

"How many have you got? Brothers and sisters, I mean."

"Two of each."

"A small loaf won't go far."

Molly was defiant in the face of Ruby's beauty and her neat dress and slippers. She hated begging, but it was that or lying awake all night listening to Gwen and Beatie crying for food.

"Can't hope to get more than a farthing."

"You don't live near here. I would have met you before if you did."

"No, over Wellsand way."

"That's a long way off. Why didn't you try to get help from your neighbours?"

Molly scowled, resenting the questions.

"'Cos they're no better off than us. I hid in a hay-cart. When I heard the driver tell the man with him they'd got to

Greenhead. I jumped off. They weren't going no further, you see."

"And you've walked all the way up here?"

"I'm used to walking. Tried some other places but folk drove me off. Well, have you got a coin to spare or not?"

"Yes, but first I'm going to take you to Waterfields."

Molly was cautious, sensing a trap.

"What's that?"

"The house where my mother and I work. You can rest for a while and we've always got a bit of something to eat. You'll get your money, don't worry."

Molly nodded. Beggars hadn't got much choice, and Ruby Travers wasn't looking down her nose at her. She seemed friendly and spoke as if she understood the problem.

Vinnie was aghast when Ruby took Molly into the kitchen. Cook's mouth dropped open and Elsie let out an exclamation of disbelief. Molly flushed scarlet, on the defensive again.

"I know I'm dirty, and not like you, but I can't help it. All of us at Brindle Mill are the same. If you want me to go, I will. I didn't ask to come here. I just wanted t' price of a small loaf."

"My dear child." Vinnie went over to Molly and put her arm round her shoulders. "It isn't like that at all, believe me. It's just that you're so ... well ... so thin and pale. Those marks ... how did you get them?"

Molly told Vinnie quite bluntly, sparing her nothing. She hadn't meant to say so much, but the woman with the light brown eyes was full of sympathy and compassion. Molly's pent-up torment poured out in a rush, stopping short of her fall from grace with Walkden.

There were tears on Vinnie's cheeks when Molly had finished.

"I'd no idea ... none of us had." Vinnie led Molly to the table. "We did hear some rumours about these cotton mills, of course, but we thought them greatly exaggerated. I fear we've been living in an ivory tower up here."

Molly didn't know what an ivory tower was. The house had

seemed ordinary enough to her from the outside. Old, of course, and very restful, but not made of a strange, unheard of material

She stared at the plate of hot-pot which Mrs. Sugarwhite had put before her.

"Is that all for me?" She couldn't quite believe such bounty. "I can't eat so much, but if you've got summat I could carry it in, I'd take it back to ma and the children."

"That's all for you and of course you can eat it." Mrs. Travers tried to smile but the effort was too great. "Cook will pack up something for you to take home to your family. You didn't mention your father."

"Dead these last twelve months."

"I'm sorry; it must be hard for you to manage."

"I said Molly could have a farthing, mother. That's all she asked for."

Vinnie shot Ruby a quick look.

"She shall have a penny or two; we can spare those easily enough. Now, dear, why don't you go and get that grey dress of yours? I reckon it'll fit Molly a treat and you've quite grown out of it."

"Couldn't." Molly stopped shovelling meat into her mouth to shake her head. "This is much more than what I expected. I only begs when the children cry till they make 'emselves sick. It's 'cos they're famished, you see. I don't hold with charity otherwise."

"Seems a pity to me not to take the dress. I was going to throw it out to-morrow." Vinnie was casual. "Didn't I say to you only the other day, Ruby, that I must make up a bundle of your old clothes and put them on a bonfire. Can't clutter the place up."

"You'd burn clothes?" Molly was incredulous. "What about your younger children?"

Mrs. Travers' eyelids dropped, veiling her thoughts.

"Ruby's my only one. Well, shall I get rid of the things? There are a few shifts and aprons and two pairs of slippers."

Molly chewed on another mouthful or two, ruminating. Then she said shyly:

"Seems wrong to do that when others could make use of 'em."

"Yes, quite wrong, and you're a very sensible girl. Ruby, come and help me put a few bits together. I've got a couple of shawls I don't wear any more. Your mother might find a use for them, that is, if she wouldn't mind accepting them."

"She wouldn't. She's very poorly; coughs all the time and can never get warm. A shawl would be like a piece of heaven to her."

Vinnie swallowed hard.

"Well, that's settled. Mrs. Sugarwhite, perhaps you and Elsie would fill that basket over there. We've got some fresh loaves, haven't we?"

Sally was blowing her nose hard, trying not to blubber.

"Aye, that we have, and there's more mutton than I know what to do with. Elsie, go and pull up a cabbage or two, and then go to the store and get some potatoes and turnips. I'll cut a slab of cake. Daresay the children will like that."

Molly was so overwhelmed by such generosity that she didn't want to take any money, but Mrs. Travers was insistent.

"Don't be foolish, my dear, you've got responsibilities. Don't be too proud either to take help when it's needed. I've done so often enough in my time."

"Have you really?"

Molly was tempted. The meal had given her fresh strength; the kindness of her new friends made her spirits rise as they had never done before.

"Yes, really. Now, you've got a long way to go so here's an extra penny. Jacob Lobbit will be by in his cart in ten minutes or so; we'll take you down to the lane. He goes in your direction every Thursday. Give that to him and tell him I asked him to give you a lift as far as he's going."

"I don't know what to say." The basket was wonderfully heavy on Molly's arm and the grey dress with its narrow velvet piping was fit for a princess. She could hardly wait to get home and put it on. " 'Thank you' don't seem enough."

"It's plenty." Vinnie and Ruby walked to the edge of the grounds with Molly, shewing her where to wait for the carter. "It's not often we get the chance to do a bit of good in this world. We're the ones who should say 'thank you', not you. If you're ever this way again come and see us, won't you? We'd like that."

Molly nodded, too overcome to say any more. When she had gone, trundling out of sight in the cart, Vinnie gave a shuddering sigh.

"Dear heavens, how can human beings be so cruel to one another? That poor child has been terribly beaten. How can the men do it?"

Ruby was young, but she knew the answer to that. She had listened very carefully to Molly's story. She took her Mother's arm and said quietly:

"They do it for money, just like they whip horses to make them move faster."

"They will have to answer to God for their sins one day."

"But not for a long while yet. Who's going to look after people like Molly and her brothers until then?"

"I don't know." Vinnie dabbed her eyes again, sick at heart. "I wish I did. Oh, love, aren't we lucky to work here at Waterfields and not at Brindle Mill? Molly has borne so much, and all she wanted was a farthing. I shall have much to be grateful for in my prayers to-night."

* * *

Ruby had wanted Mrs. Pittaway to live forever, but the Almighty and Albina herself had other ideas.

A month after Ruby and Vinnie had met Molly, Albina put her affairs in order and called in a friendly neighbour. She gave him instructions which made him scratch his head in perplexity. Mrs. Pittaway looked well enough to him, and he told his wife he thought the old girl must be going funny in the head.

Two days later, Albina died in her sleep. Her face was peaceful and somehow satisfied. She'd lived her life the way she'd wanted to, and had died in the same way.

When the loom and other things had been taken up to the large attic, Ruby sat down on her bed to open the polished wooden box which had come with them. She stared at the twenty golden sovereigns in disbelief and when she picked up the three rings her amazement was even greater. They didn't look cheap or tawdry. The diamond was like a piece of ice which had been set on fire; the ruby had witchcraft in its depths; the emerald was large and flawless. When she had stacked her treasure under some clothes in the chest, she went to speak to her mother.

"She left me more than I expected," she said calmly, although she was bubbling with excitement inside. She was rich now, but one thing had to be made very plain to Vinnie. "I want you to promise me something."

Mrs. Travers didn't ask what her daughter's inheritance was. She didn't think it could be all that much and Ruby was a sensible girl. She'd look after it, whatever it was, and was entitled to privacy.

"What, dear?"

Ruby's lips hardened and her eyes met Vinnie's, demanding her mother's full attention.

"Cuddy is not to know about my legacy. Give me your word you'll never mention it to him."

Mrs. Travers wavered, then she nodded. She wished Ruby was on better terms with her uncle, but she really couldn't blame the girl. Cuddy wasn't the boy she had reared; he'd changed into a completely different person. Besides, his niece owed him nothing. The past wasn't her responsibility.

"All right, if you say so, but Ruby."

"Yes?"

"I know you don't like Cuddy, but before life battered him so, he was a dear. And don't forget …"

Ruby waited, expecting more excuses to be made for Dalton, but Mrs. Travers broke off, bowing her head.

"Perhaps he was, but now he's disgusting."

"Not really, but whatever you feel about him you wouldn't do anything to hurt him, would you?"

"Of course not; how could I?"

"Well, I suppose what I really mean is if he needed help, and I wasn't here, you'd do what you could, wouldn't you?"

"Depends."

"No." Vinnie's voice broke. "Please give me a promise to match mine. Tell me you'd not see him suffer if I wasn't here to do what was needed."

"Mother, don't talk like that. You're young."

"I know, but I'm mortal, too. It would mean so much to me. Say you'd help him."

Reluctantly Ruby gave in. She could see how much it meant to Vinnie and a word or two didn't hurt. Vinnie would live for years and Cuddy was wily enough to keep himself out of trouble.

"All right, I promise. I'll help, if I have to, provided you stop talking about not being here."

Vinnie gave a quick sigh of relief.

"Yes, I will, and thank you. Now, enough of sad thoughts. Let's have a glass of cider and drink a toast to my sweet and wealthy daughter."

* * *

In the spring of 1793, when Ruby was nineteen years old and lovelier than ever, Vinnie Travers caught a chill and was dead within the week.

The shock hit Ruby hard, for Vinnie had been the pivot of her existence. She stood by the graveside, sad and forlorn, but she din't weep. Her mother wouldn't have wanted her to do that in public. Tears were for when one was by oneself and had to be shed at night.

She went back to Waterfields with cook and Janet, the new scullerymaid. Elsie had left some two years before and Ruby missed her. Janet was a whiner and not addicted to work.

After a cup of chocolate and a currant cake, which Sally Sugarwhite had baked as a mark of respect to her friend, Ruby went up to the attic and started to weave. She was soothed by the regular flowing movement of the shuttle, and by the swinging batten which forced the weft into a perfectly straight line, the reed ensuring that as each blow was struck, every warp end was correctly placed.

She had done well since she had started on her own. Every spare moment had been spent making fine muslins and cottons, and the journeymen went out of their way to call at Waterfields to pick up the finished materials. It was much sought after and usually fetched three shillings and sixpence a yard.

Ruby waited a week before approaching Sir Warren with her proposal. It wasn't only a question of regard for Vinnie's memory. She had seen the sadness in Askwith during the previous few days. She wasn't sure of its cause but, as he had no family to worry about, she assumed he was beset by fresh financial problems. What she was going to suggest wouldn't solve all his difficulties, but every little helped.

He gave her his slow, engaging smile as she made a respectful bob. For a second or two she thought he was going to say something. Words seemed to hover round his lips but, as usual, he was indecisive. He just inclined his head and it was left to Ruby to break the silence.

When he had heard her out he said faintly:

"You? My housekeeper? My dear, you are much too young."

"I'm nineteen, sir, and I know exactly how the place has to be run. I wouldn't want as much as you paid mother, so that will make things easier."

He still shook his head, looking more appalled than ever. Ruby was patient with him. After all, Vinnie had been his servant for many years. They had seen one another every day, even if they had only been discussing the limited menu, or how much it would cost to mend a broken window. In his own way, he probably missed her too.

"I can do it, I know I can."

"But it ... it wouldn't be proper. No, no, it's quite impossible."

It took nearly twenty minutes to coax Askwith into an acceptance of the plan. He was weak and Ruby very determined. In addition, the thought of dealing with a strange housekeeper had been bothering him since Vinnie's death.

"Well, we can try it I suppose," he said at last, knowing he was beaten. "What about cook and the girl? Will they mind working under you?"

"Mrs. Sugarwhite won't, and Janet will do as she's told."

Ruby named the wage she thought appropriate, enquired what her master wanted for his evening meal, and then left him looking after her helplessly. He knew he'd done the wrong thing, but Ruby had been so self-possessed, efficient and remorseless as she went after her goal that he'd been quite unable to stand up to her.

When Ruby got back to the kitchen her uncle was waiting for her. She gave him a very frosty look and said curtly:

"I sent a message to you at that gipsy camp about mother. Why weren't you at the funeral?"

"I were ill again."

"Intoxicated, more like. You're despicable. Surely you could have spared her half an hour of your miserable life?"

"'Ere, you've no right to talk to me that way."

"If you don't like the way I speak to you, you have your remedy. Get out."

There was a very marked difference in his niece from the last time he had seen her and Cuddy changed his tune rapidly. There was a new glint in her eye; an unforgiving line to her mouth.

"Give us a bite to eat, then I'll go. I'll need a bit of money. Down on my luck and I can't get work."

Ruby inspected him from head to toe. This wasn't the kind of help of which her mother had spoken. They had only discussed the matter briefly, but his customary cadging hadn't been the cause of Vinnie's anxiety.

"You can't get work because you don't look for it. If you want food, go and earn enough to buy some. You'll get neither crust nor copper from me, Cuddy Dalton. I'm not my mother, and you just remember that. Now get off with you, I'm busy."

He cursed and wheedled, but Ruby stood rock-firm.

"Out," she repeated and opened the door. "You're not in trouble, so don't pretend you are. All that's the matter with you is that every bone in your body is idle."

She slammed the door shut behind him, not even listening to the string of ripe imprecations which filtered through the crack. When and if the need came, she'd keep her promise to her mother. Meanwhile, she had other things to do and she called to Sally Sugarwhite and Janet who were cleaning out the larder.

They came hurriedly, for her tone brooked no delay. Cook was flushed and perspiring as a result of her scrubbing; Janet looked sulky as usual.

"I have some news for you," said Ruby crisply, starting as she meant to go on. "Sir Warren has just appointed me to be the new housekeeper. I'm sure we shall get along splendidly, and see that the master is cared for as in the past. Janet, go back and finish the larder. I want to talk to Mrs. Sugarwhite."

"Don't see why I've got to do it all on me own, and no one said owt about you being housekeeper when I comes here."

"No, but I'm telling you now. Either get on with that scrubbing or put your hat on and go home. I don't much mind which you do, but don't waste my time."

Janet flounced off, muttering under her breath, and Ruby relaxed as she gave Sally a wink.

"Don't worry, Mrs. Sugarwhite," she said with a slight giggle. "I had to shew that little piece who is going to give the orders around here. Sit down, you look fit to drop. I'll make us a cup of tea and we'll have one of your Banbury cakes to celebrate. Master couldn't make up his mind whether he wanted pork or suet pudding to-night, or that tasty veal dish you make. Suppose there's nothing for it; we shall have to make up his mind for him. Well, what do you think would be best?"

"He's very partial to veal."

"Then veal it shall be."

"If you think that's all right."

"I shall leave all the cooking and catering to you and it couldn't be in better hands. Here's your cup. I'm sure I'm going to manage all right, don't you?"

Sally took a bite out of her Banbury cake. They'd come out really well, if she did say so herself. Then she looked at Ruby. Funny not to have Mrs. Travers there any more, but the gleam in the new housekeeper's eye told her all she wanted to know.

"Aye, lass, you'll do. If you've put your mind to it, nothing's going to stop you, and I'll help all I can."

"I know you will." Ruby's smile made Sally feel warm inside. "Couldn't do it without you. Now, do you think I'd get very fat if I had another cake? I think I'll chance it, for they're quite the best you've ever made. Now, about the marketing …"

Sally kept her smile to herself. Ruby might look and sound like a small girl playing mother, but she'd be as good at her job as her mother had been. Whatever Ruby Travers set her hand to she would do and do it well. Failure was not a word which Vinnie's daughter understood.

THREE

"No, there is no question in my mind. Stratton must leave London without delay."

Martin Clare, Marquis of Harworth, turned from the window to answer the query from his lawyer, Oscar Edington. The marquis was a man of infinite sophistication and poise, with bright, penetrating eyes, a bold nose and jaw which gave some indication of his iron will.

His attire was always immaculate, extremely expensive, and in the height of fashion. He used his quizzing glass without mercy against those who bored or offended him, his tongue as lethal as any sword when moved to irritation. He was vastly rich, had the king's ear, and was acknowledged as one of the foremost leaders of the *haut monde*.

"If you think that best."

His lordship's well-shaped mouth grew even harder than normal.

"It's the only way. Until eight months ago Sebastian was everything a father could wish to find in a son. Then he fell in with this group of young men and is now on the verge of moral bankruptcy. These creatures are depraved, vicious and dissolute and they're dragging Stratton down into the sewers with them. It is the pattern of my grandfather's life all over again."

Edington cleared his throat. He had never seen worry in the marquis before. It was there that morning, carefully controlled, but clear enough.

"I didn't know your grandfather, of course."

"You were lucky." Clare was terse. "He ended up in a madhouse, diseased, sodden with drink, afflicted by syphilis and prone to outbursts of such filth and violence that even the hardened attendants in the asylum blenched. I will not stand by and see Sebastian go the same way. I shall order him out of town immediately. The question is, where to send him."

The lawyer fingered his chin. He understood Clare's alarm, for the Earl of Stratton's reputation had not escaped his own ears.

"There is a small property in Lancashire, my lord, at Tockfold. You may recall your late cousin left you several in that area. For some reason, one of the houses wasn't sold."

The marquis's smile was satanic.

"A most excellent suggestion, m'dear fellow. Even Stratton can't get into mischief in a wilderness like that. I shall give him the barest allowance to live on, and certainly not enough to pay vintners' bills, gambling dues, or for the services of harlots to entertain him. Find some reliable agent to keep an eye on him, though. I want to know what he's doing, but make sure he doesn't find out he's being watched. He may be a rakehell, but he's not a fool. You'd better wait in the library. He's due at any moment and what I have to say to him is best done in private."

When Edington had withdrawn, a flunkey came to announce the arrival of the Earl of Stratton. Slowly the marquis raised his quizzing glass, watching his son cross the room.

If Sebastian Clare was about to topple over into the bottomless pit for his sins he shewed little sign of it. He was tall, lean and broad-shouldered, moving with an almost feline grace. His dark hair was curled about his head à la Brutus; his face was moulded in near-perfect lines. To gild the lily, the earl had chosen to wear a drab-olive coat, cut away in front, with mere tails behind which terminated above the knees. His waistcoats was of finest silk, his stock delicate lawn, the ruffles at his wrists made of the best lace money could buy. His small-clothes were cream-coloured, the breeches hugging long, sinewy legs. The polish of his boots with turned-over tops was beyond reproach; his gloves were made of the very best York tan.

He made his bow to his father and then straightened up to face what was clearly going to be a most uncomfortable half-hour. His sire's summons had been couched in terms brief but cogent and Sebastian had pulled a face when he read the contents of the note.

He donned his most arrogant air, using a bland stare to conceal some trepidation and a very uneasy conscience. It was quite a while since he had taken stock of himself. His father's letter had caused him to make a quick review of recent events and they proved far from savoury. He had felt shame, a sensation which had not troubled him for a long time, and he didn't like it.

The last batch of tradesmen's bills had been heavy, his gambling debts pressing and quite shattering in their size. One of his cronies had raped a gently-bred young female; another had been caught cheating at cards. A third had run away from an outraged husband, leaving the woman involved to face the music alone.

Finally, the earl himself had fought a duel, injuring his opponent. That in itself was no disgrace, but Stratton was well-aware that he had been in his cups when he had issued the challenge. He was sure his father would have heard about the latter incident; nothing ever escaped the marquis.

He gritted his teeth at his father's drawl, knowing of old that it meant real trouble, listening in silence as his shortcomings were listed in detail. The marquis's assessment of his son's boon companions didn't help either. Every shaft went home like a well-shot arrow.

Finally Sebastian was stung into a response.

"I regret that you find me so unworthy, my lord, but from what I have heard you were not exactly a monk when you were my age."

The marquis was scathing.

"No, but I grew up, and at no time did I behave like a degenerate lout. I am not prepared to prolong this discussion, nor enter into an argument with you. I propose to put an end to your excesses here and now."

"Really?" The earl appeared to be on the point of yawning, but his nerve-ends had begun to twitch. "Now how, I wonder, do you propose to do that?"

"Very simply, and watch your tongue when you speak to me. I shall send you to Tockfold in Lancashire, where I have a small house. Your allowance will be minimal; just sufficient for essential food and wages for a woman to cook and clean for you.

If the earl had not been such an experienced card player he might have betrayed his horror at his father's decision. As it was, he merely drew a gold snuff-box from his waistcoat pocket and took a pinch with an easy, practised flick of the wrist.

"I can hardly believe you are serious. You can't ask such a thing of me."

"I am not asking you," returned the marquis coldly. "I am telling you. You will leave to-day for Tockfold and you will stay there for a year."

"You wouldn't dare!"

As soon as Sebastian said it he knew he had made a mistake, biting his lip as the marquis raised his head to give him a long, unwavering look.

"What did you say, Stratton? I think I must have misheard you, for I cannot conceive that you would be so foolhardy as to utter the words which seemed to reach my ears."

"I ask your pardon, my lord, but this is totally absurd. What can I do in Tockfold for twelve months?"

"I don't particularly care." Clare was indifferent. "I can be assured that you will not be able to drink heavily, if at all; gamble; run a stable of fast horses, or sleep with a different woman every night."

"Even I can't manage such a feat." The earl was trying to

pull himself together without his father noticing it, aghast at the prospect which lay before him. At first, he hadn't believed the marquis intended to impose such draconian measures, but a glance at the latter's face shewed how wrong he had been. "And if I have to go, I must take Wallis with me. I can't face the early mornings without a valet."

"I don't see why not. It's time you learned to dress yourself, but you may do as you please. Just bear in mind that his remuneration will come out of an already limited income."

"Damn it!" Stratton's caution was quickly forgotten when the full extent of the disaster began to dawn on him. "I've a mind to find a disgustingly rich woman of low ancestry and marry her."

"I hope I never hear that you are considering such a contemptible move." Clare's tone was very steely. "But if you try to match yourself with a woman not of our world I'll stop you. Make no mistake about that. You are my only son and you bear a proud name. You've done your best to drag it through the mire, but a mèsalliance I will not tolerate."

Sebastian abandoned that threat rather hastily, realising the folly of pursuing such a line. He tried another tactic.

"You cannot force me to agree to this plan."

"Indeed I can," replied the marquis smoothly. "If you don't leave for Lancashire to-day, and stay there until I give you leave to return, you won't get another penny from me. As the estate is entailed, I fear you will inherit everything when I die, but that will not be for a long while yet. How do you fancy being a poor man for the next twenty years?"

The earl grew white about the month, his grey eyes burning with a rage he dared not unleash.

"My grandmother won't live that long. When she dies, I shall have her fortune."

"Your maternal grandmother has the constitution of an ox. Don't bank on any assistance arising from her early demise. Well?"

Quite suddenly the earl's anger collapsed. His father held

all the trumps and was more than capable of using them. Also, he was bound to admit that he had rather asked for it. He hadn't meant to follow Lord Dacre, Sir Peter Whyte and the others into such scandalous escapades. It had just happened. Now he had to pay for his carelessness and lack of judgment.

"It seems I have no choice." Sebastian was cursing inwardly. "That being so and, since you are so set upon me departing immediately, I had better go and pack. I assume I may be permitted to take one of my own phaetons with me?"

Clare gave a thin smile.

"You will travel by post-chaise to your destination. I will arrange for a modest, second-hand curricle to be purchased and delivered to you. You may have two horses as well. They won't be fliers, like your bays, but they'll trot along fast enough for a gentleman in reduced circumstances."

Sebastian drew a deep breath, but he knew he was beaten.

"And my debts, my lord?"

"I shall pay them, of course. Have all the bills sent round to me."

"I'm obliged, sir."

Stratton made a leg in the most formal of manners and left the room, closing the door loudly behind him.

"I fear Sebastian is somewhat annoyed," said the marquis to Edington over a glass of claret. "Ah well, it can't be helped. He's my only child and more important to me than my own life."

"Quite, my lord."

"Still, I hope he comes to his senses in six months rather than twelve. It's ridiculous, I know, but I'm very much afraid I'm going to miss that impudent young devil."

* * *

"This place is no better than a box with a lid on it," said Stratton fretfully to Wallis, his manservant and close confidant. "I shall go mad shut up in here for a year."

Walis gave a murmur of sympathy. He had had to listen to a veritable tirade from his master as they had drive away from the capital, soothing the earl with an assurance that he himself was very nicely placed and needed no wages until better times came again.

As soon as the marquis's decree had been made known to him, Wallis had got busy. In the space of two hours he had procured three well-cut but modest outfits, explaining patiently to the outraged Stratton that he would cause a furore in a quiet Lancashire village, dressed as if he were about to set off for White's or Bond Street.

He had also advised Sebastian to drop his title, a suggestion which Stratton accepted gloomily. Wallis had been right, of course, on all counts. He would have to lie low for a while and the trappings of a beau, or a hint of his lineage, would be fatal.

"It is a bit cramped." Wallis was thoughtful. "Perhaps we can get rid of some of the furniture."

"Furniture! It's only fit for firewood."

"I've found a woman to clean and prepare the meals, my lord."

"Mr. Clare."

"Ah yes, of course; forgive me. She seemed very suitable of me. A motherly body who'll do us well, I fancy. Her name is Mrs. Offer."

"Can I afford her?"

"Most certainly. Please put all such worries out of your head, my ... er ... sir. I will look after the money."

"Such as it is. Oh damn my father! I suppose we've nothing to drink but water?"

"As a matter of fact, I did take the precaution of filling an extra clothes basket with some liquid refreshment. I thought it might come in useful!"

Sebastian gave Wallis a quick grin.

"You're a cunning knave. Let's hope my father doesn't find out what you did."

"He won't." The valet was smug. "I was most careful to

ensure that nobody was about."

"Thank God. I'll have a large brandy."

Two weeks later Wallis poured another generous measure of cognac, for he had news to impart which he did not think the earl was going to like at all.

"We have received a message from Lady Annora," he said, and almost thrust the glass into the earl's hand.

Lady Annora Eyre was a society beauty of high renown. Wallis had to admit that she had looks, style, and was of irreproachable ancestry. Unfortunately, she was also unscrupulous, selfish, ill-tempered and sometimes downright dangerous. He felt it was a pity she had taken it into her head to fall hopelessly in love with the earl. Normally, she treated her devoted admirers with scorn, discarding them as she would throw away a hat of which she had grown tired. With Sebastian it was different. Even the critical valet could see her love for his master was genuine, but it was most inconvenient for she wasn't at all the type of woman his lordship should contemplate taking as his partner in life.

"Christ, already? If she's imploring me to go back to town she's going to be unlucky."

"Not back to London. She has taken a house at Raygreen."

"Where the hell is that?"

"Not very far away, I fear."

The earl gazed at Wallis as if he were a snake about to strike him dead.

"You don't mean to say she's followed me up here?"

"I'm afraid so, sir. She wants you to go and see her to-morrow."

The earl slumped back in his chair and held out his glass to be refilled.

"Is there no end to the tribulations besetting me? Isn't it bad enough that I've been driven from civilisation to this ... this backwater? Must I now be pestered by a woman I no longer give tuppence for?"

"You seemed to be quite enamoured of her at one time, if I may say so."

"I was quite madly in love with her, but she wouldn't go to bed with me."

"Well naturally she wouldn't. She wants to marry you. If she'd played the harlot, you wouldn't have offered for her."

"I wasn't going to offer for her anyway." Sebastian was sour. "It wasn't that kind of relationship. "Blast her! Can I refuse to go?"

"Rather unwise, I'd think." Wallis was shaking his head. "She could soon make known your true identity if she chose to be difficult."

"And she would be. Yes, you're right; I'll have to go. I must keep her sweet somehow if I want her silence. Why on earth doesn't she leave me alone?"

"I was told she is besotted with you. It was a most reliable source."

"Oh God! How did she find out where I was going?"

"That will remain one of life's little mysteries, but servants have wagging tongues and long ears."

"Whoever babbled to Annora should have both cut off and also his …"

"Indeed, sir, and now I must make sure Mrs. Offer has started to prepare your luncheon. Perhaps it would be as well if you took a walk to give yourself an appetite."

"If I thought I'd die quickly enough I wouldn't let a crumb pass my lips. Any measures would be worth trying to get out of this place."

"The curricle then, sir?"

"Have you seen it?"

"Well yes, when it arrived this morning."

"And the creatures his lordship chose to describe as horses?"

"Those, too."

Sebastian unwound his tall frame from the chair and adjusted his stock.

"Well, I suppose I've got to get used to them since they're

all I've got or likely to have in the foreseeable future. If I'm not back in an hour send a search party out for me. I shall either be lost on these benighted moors, or the beasts will have died of old age and left me stranded."

Wallis watched his master stride down the path which led to a small stable. He felt for the earl, but secretly he was vastly relieved that the marquis had taken action at last. The company Stratton had been keeping would have led to his undoing, had his father not put his foot down. It really was all for the best, tetchy thought the earl had become.

Lady Annora Eyre was tiresome. Lord Dacre, Peter Whyte and Charles de Vere were beyond the pale, and there was a good stock of wine and spirits by way of solace for the earl.

Wallis gave a faint, satisfied smile and went into the poky kitchen to see what Mrs. Agatha Offer was up to.

* * *

"But, dearest, of course I had to come. As soon as I learned what had happened I arranged to stay in this house which belongs to a friend of mine. It isn't what I'm used to, of course, but what does that matter as long as I'm near you?"

Stratton looked down at Lady Annora Eyre, wondering whatever had made him kneel in supplication at her feet for so many months. It was true, of course, that her hair shone like pure gold, and that her eyes were large, limpid, and as blue as the skies. Her full lips invited kisses, her skin was flawless and coloured like an apricot.

She wore an open robe of yellow satin that day, with long, tight sleeves and a gossamer-thin buffon which made a delicious mystery of her breasts.

"Who told you? Damn it, I've only been here for a fortnight."

Annora smiled lovingly.

"I can't remember. Probably Farrow heard it from one of your servants."

The earl shot Farrow, Lady Eyre's personal maid, a far

from friendly glance. He had never liked the woman. She was stout, and square-built, with glassy eyes which missed nothing, and a mouth like a trap.

"Come and sit down. Farrow, you may go."

The woman bobbed without the slightest hint of deference. She didn't mind being sent off. Later, when she was undressing her mistress and taking the ornaments out of her hair, the latter would tell her everything. Her ladyship needed someone to whom she could unburden herself; a person who would listen and sympathise when needs be. In return, she shared her most intimate secrets. Farrow had no life of her own, but she existed vicariously and quite happily through Annora's.

The latest man to ply Annora with jewels and other costly gifts was the low born Lionel Whitcombe. Normally Farrow had no time for those engaged in trade; they were common as muck and not nearly good enough for her mistress. However, it was beyond dispute that Whitcombe was not only generous to her ladyship. He was very free with his sovereigns as far as she, Farrow, was concerned and that made him just acceptable. She had a great weakness for gin and gin cost money.

So far, the merchant had not got beyond the drawing-room when he had made his frequent trips to London. Lady Annora wanted to marry Stratton and if she were to become Whitcombe's mistress, and the earl found out about it, her chances of achieving her objective would be at an end. Now they were in Lancashire they were bound to see more of the merchant. He would disperse even more largesse, and Farrow wasn't complaining about their move.

"Well, now tell me all about it. At first I could hardly believe your father had sent you into exile for so long." Annora feasted her eyes on Sebastian, wishing he would sit next to her. "Why did he do it?"

"He didn't like the company I was keeping." Sebastian was short. "He is bringing me to heel by making me live in a house no bigger than a shepherd's cottage. It smells like a sty and there isn't room to move. He's cut my allowance to a mere pittance, so I can't gamble, keep a stable, or even eat what I want to. Apart from Wallis, I've only one servant to cook and clean. It's quite intolerable."

Annora didn't think so, for it almost delivered the earl into her hands, but she said soothingly:

"You can eat whatever you like when you're here, my sweet."

"Thank you, but that hardly solves the problem, does it?"

"Perhaps not, but I've a solution which would."

The earl recognised the purr in her tone and became wary. He hadn't meant to divulge quite so much to Annora, but he was still smarting over his new and uncomfortable lifestyle.

"Oh? I can think of nothing which would enlarge either my residence or my income."

"I can." Her need for him was growing by the minute. He was so very handsome and he made her heart beat as fast as a foolish maiden over her first love. "You could marry me. Once you're my husband, I'll buy the world for you if you want it. My poor departed George left me quite abominably rich. You shall have a castle to live in, a hundred horses if you've a mind for them, a different outfit for every day of the year, and you can gamble for any stakes you like, provided, of course, you come to my bed each night."

Sebastian felt waves of shock run through him as if he'd been struck by lightning, although he gave no outward sign of what she had done to him.

Nothing the marquis had said had gone home as surely as Annora's offer to buy him as her husband. That was how she saw him. A weak-kneed fop who would become a woman's plaything in exchange for bodily comforts. It made him feel completely degraded. He wanted to slap her across the face for daring to make such a proposal; to stalk out of the house shouting that he would never return. It wasn't possible, of course, as Wallis had pointed out. He had to keep Annora quiet and therefore reasonably happy. It left an even nastier taste in his mouth as he hunted round for an appropriate response.

"Well, my lord?"

"I'm not using my title." He was glad of the brief reprieve. "I am Mr. Sebastian Clare whilst I'm here in this ghastly place."

"Of course, so sensible. I'll be sure to remember that. It may have its advantages, too. We shall be free to amuse ourselves as we like."

"I doubt it. You shouldn't have followed me here. You'll be as bored as I am."

He saw the light change behing her eyes and cursed. He would have to be more careful if he wanted Annora's co-operation.

"That is to say, my dear, I don't like the idea of you suffering the same privations as I have to."

Her irritation was gone, her smile as warm as ever.

"I shan't, never fear. Will you dine with me to-morrow?"

He wanted to tell her to go to perdition, but he found himself agreeing reluctantly as he rose to make his bow.

She laid down her fan, coming to stand very close to him so that his nose was assaulted by her cloying perfume. There was a tiger there, waiting to spring out at him.

"Until to-morrow then, dear Sebastian. You may kiss me, if you wish, and think about my suggestion, won't you? It really would be the answer to everything."

He put as much enthusiasm into his task as he could muster and then almost ran from the house. The horse he was riding wasn't up to the speed he was demanding of it and after a few miles it stumbled, throwing him heavily.

Ruby Travers was on her way back from Burnley Market. It was a fine day and she had decided to walk. She liked to make the household purchases herself, watching the pennies as Albina Pittaway had told her to do, and making sure she got the best value for her outlay.

When she saw the rider fall she let her baskets go flying, running to his side, an exclamation of dismay on her lips.

When she saw his face, the consternation died in a second and something else took its place.

He wasn't fair-haired and solidly built. He was lean and elegant, with thin, strong hands. His eyes were grey, not blue, and there was no humour about the line of his mouth.

As Ruby knelt there she knew it didn't matter. In one tiny fraction of time her world had turned upside down, and she knew why. She had only played at being in love before; this was the real thing. She wasn't sure why she was so certain; she just was. She wanted to rest her hand against his cheek and tell him of her feelings. She yearned to lean forward and touch his mouth with her own, even though she had only just that second encountered him.

To stop herself doing something which would shame her for ever she said quickly:

"Sir, are you hurt?"

The earl had been slightly stunned by his fall, but his head cleared as she spoke. Then he looked at his rescuer, his answer dying on his tongue as he stared at the girl bending over him.

Her hair was like black satin, her eyes dark brown and luminous, as if a candle was burning behind them. Although her complexion was pale it had the glow of health about it, emphasized by the wash of colour along the cheekbones. She had a small, delicate nose and a mouth which made his heart race as if he had been running fast for a long time.

When she helped him to his feet he found she only reached to his shoulder. It made her seem vulnerable, needing his protection. She had a body both slender and sensual. The swell of her breasts and tiny waist made him feel as if he had consumed the total stock of intoxicants which Wallis had brought from London. Her nearness was the most potent aphrodisiac he had ever known, and it was then that he realised what had happened to him.

When the words came, he did not know whether he had spoken them aloud or not. He held her gaze with his, feeling as if he had been born anew.

"You are the beginning of my life," he said very softly. "I will love you from this moment on until my ending."

"Sir?" Ruby hadn't caught what he had said. It was just a whisper, but she understood his expression well enough. It was a miracle, for she read in him her own fierce longing and desire. "Did you say something?"

He was relieved that it was only his heart which had cried out to her. If he had really voiced such an absurdity, she would have thought him mad. Yet perhaps she wouldn't, for in the wide, beautiful eyes he could see love just like his own. However, he had to be certain before he made a fool of himself and he shook his head, denying the oath he had just made.

"No, no, it was nothing. I was simply berating myself for such clumsiness."

She hadn't looked away and it felt as if he was scanning her soul, knowing that she had recognized his lie.

"I'm Sebastian Clare," he said, trying to concentrate on everyday things. "I was making for Tockfold. It appears that I shall have to walk the rest of the way since my horse has deserted me."

Ruby didn't hesitate. It might be the only chance she would ever have of being with him for a little while and she took it firmly with both hands.

"I work at Waterfields, not far off. You've grazed your face, you know. Come with me and let me bathe it and give you some refreshment. I'm sure we can find another horse for you." She gave a sudden smile and he was bewitched. "I'm afraid it will be rather an old one and not very fast. Does that matter?"

"Not in the least; mine was just the same. But I can't put you to so much trouble, Miss ... ?"

"I'm Ruby Travers, housekeeper to Sir Warren Askwith. He's away on business for two days, otherwise he would have insisted on offering you his hospitality. Please do come."

It had never occured to him to refuse the invitation, once

given. He wanted to spend as long as possible with Ruby, although he accepted with a sinking heart that this ecstatic interlude in his life would be of short duration. However deeply he loved her, and absurdly he did, his father would not permit marriage. There was no alternative, for he would never use her as he'd used his high-born, promiscuous mistresses.

They talked easily and without shyness or reserve. It seemed to them that they had known one another for a long time, both conscious that it was more than a new friendship which they shared. Once or twice Ruby stopped to give silent thanks to her guardian angel that Sally and Janet had gone to the village. It would have been too dreadful if they had been there to spoil things.

Under her supreme happiness there was a great sadness. Clearly, Sebastian Clare was a gentleman. Not, perhaps, a rich one. His clothes were plain for all that he wore them with such an air, but she wasn't of his world and never would be. The joy of being with him would be a fleeting thing, but she believed in making the most of the present, leaving tears to the future.

She attended to his bruises, gave him a glass of wine from the meagre stock in his dining-room, and cut him a piece of seed cake. He followed every movement she made, basking in her solicitude which never became fussiness. He wanted to be with her for the rest of his days so that she could care for him as she was doing now. It was impossible so, like Ruby, he made the best of what the gods had granted him.

"I must go," he said finally, when there was no longer any excuse to tarry. "You've been so kind, Miss Travers."

"Most people call me Ruby, sir. If you won't think me too forward, perhaps you would like to do the same."

"I would indeed. May I dare to hope that you will call me Sebastian?"

She frowned as she faced up to realities.

"It isn't quite the same thing, is it?"

They shared the undeniable truth for a moment or two,

then let it slide away, for neither wanted to acknowledge it.

"Perhaps not, but please consider the idea."

"I may not see you again."

His lips curved in a way which made Ruby feel as though he had embraced her, warmth tingling down to her toes.

"You will, Ruby, I promise you."

Her beam dazzled him and he thought it was just as well that she was leading him outside to where an ancient mare awaited him. In the blissful cocoon of the kitchen he might well have taken her in his arms and kissed her, and it wasn't time for that yet.

Ruby watched him ride away, wanting to sing aloud. She didn't think she would be going to Trawley Dale any more. That contained only a childhood fantasy which had blown away as soon as she had seen Sebastian's face.

"You're perky to-day," said cook later, as she began to make the pastry for a meat pie. "If I didn't know better I'd think you were in love."

Ruby laughed, hugging her secret to herself.

"What nonsense; I'm just in a good mood. Who wouldn't be on such a glorious day as this? Oh, Mrs. Sugarwhite, isn't this the very best day you've ever known?"

FOUR

By some strange quirk of fate, love came into Molly Caudle's life at almost the same time as Ruby met the Earl of Stratton.

Her lot hadn't improved much. Her mother had died two years before, leaving her responsible for her younger brothers and sisters. She hated to be away from Gwen and Beatie for so many hours, but there was no alternative. Sometimes the neighbours remembered to look in on the girls; mostly they forgot their existence, having too many worries of her own.

The only relief had been the death of Ham Walkden in a fight some three months after he had lain with her. She was thankful that he had gone, for he had kept up his demands and, for Timmy's sake, she had had to agree. She was quicker now, and more skilful, thus getting fewer beatings. Timmy and Angus were not so lucky and she still wept when they fell foul of the overseers and were flogged until they were half-insensible.

When she first saw Bertram Corbin her heart did a complete somersault. It wasn't that he was handsome. He was short and wiry, with brown eyes, a blunt nose and a kindly mouth. His clothes were shabby, his boots without proper soles, but none of that mattered to Molly. She would have given anything to talk to him but, of course, it was his place to speak first.

After he had been there three days, Bertram decided to venture an approach to the girl who carried the flyers to the rollers. She was the prettiest thing he had ever seen and her blue eyes made him quite dizzy when she cast a shy glance in his direction. She was very poor, like him, and it hurt to see the thinness of her body. Black bread and rancid bacon provided by the mill manager gave little nourishment and often Molly and the others were too tired to eat anyway.

With his first week's wages Bertram bought a wheaten loaf. It made quite a hole in his spare money, but he didn't care. He cut some slices carefully, begging a scrape of butter from the woman with whom he lodged, wrapping up the provender and tucking it in his coat pocket.

When he walked over to Molly in the dinner break she blushed furiously. It was what she had been praying for ever since he had arrived at Brindle Mill, but now that he was standing in front of her she had no idea what to say.

He saw her embarrassment and tried to put her at ease.

"Mind if I sit here for a while?"

Molly shook her head silently, feeling quite giddy as he took his place beside her. She watched him unwrap the bread, looking at it in astonishment. He grinned, pleased because he had been able to bring her a small treat.

"Can't starve, can we? Here, have a bit."

"I ... I mustn't." She was angry with herself for stammering. He would think her witless and go away, so she tried to calm herself down. "I couldn't take your food. Wouldn't be fair."

Bertram considerd her pallor, the wonder of her hair, and the bloodless but desirable lips which made him feel queer inside. If they had been born into a different world there would have been time for gradual acquaintanceship which, hopefully, would turn to courtship. But there was neither time nor opportunity. Their lives were wound round the mill as surely as cotton round a bobbin. If they were to share anything he would have to take the plunge and he did so without further ado.

"It 'ud be fair enough, seeing I bought the loaf special for you."

Her eyes met his, widening in a mixture of puzzlement and hope.

"For me?"

"Aye. A girl like you should have better 'un what you've got there. Here, take this. We'll have to be back at work soon enough."

She murmured her thanks and he watched her take her first bite, hating the ravenous hunger in her. It had been bad enough watching the children scavenging for scraps in the pig-trough which belonged to the manager. Molly's plight was far worse to him.

"Where do you live?"

"Wellsand."

"Now that's a funny thing. I lodge not far from there myself. Alone, are you?"

"No, I've got brothers and sisters to care for. Ma died some time ago. You see ..."

In the space of ten minutes Corbin had learned all the relevant facts of Molly's life. The only thing which she left out of her tale was Ham, for she couldn't bear the thought of Bertram finding out about her disgrace. The other girls wouldn't let her down; they all stuck together in their misery.

Even though his own existence hadn't been much easier, her story sickened Corbin. She was so young and yet so resolute, not in the least sorry for herself and standing up to knock after knock.

"Time's almost up and you don't know owt about me. What do you say to a walk come Sunday? I'll tell you about myself then."

"I'm sorry, I didn't mean to talk so much." Molly was stricken by her selfishness. "I oughtn't to have gone on so."

"Don't moither yourself; I asked. Well, what about Sunday?"

"There are the children ..." She longed to say yes, praying he would press her. "I've got to do the cleaning, too. Don't know that I ought to."

He read her easily and felt a glow in his heart. She wanted to go with him; all he had to do was to push.

"Reckon you should, seeing you've chattered so much I 'aven't got a word in edgewise, and cleaning can wait."

Suddenly they were laughing. Molly had never really known what laughter was and it was a peculiar sensation. But it was wonderful, too, and she nodded.

"All right. Seems I owes you that."

She told him where to pick her up and then went back to the flyers feeling as if she were walking on air.

For the first time ever she could see some purpose in God's plan and in two days time she would have Bertram to herself. She didn't feel tired any more and her aches seemed to have gone. There were still six hours to go, but she didn't care.

Nothing mattered now that she was going to walk out with Bertram Corbin.

* * *

Ruby sat and looked at the lawyer on the other side of the desk. She wore the black dress she'd made to attend Vinnie's funeral, and a fresh white apron. She hadn't expected to have to go into mourning again so soon, and when a villager had come running to the house with the dire news that Askwith had fallen and broken his neck, she had been shocked to the core.

For the preceding two months she had been in heaven. All day she thought about Sebastian Clare and at night she dreamed of him. She was careful not to let cook or Janet see her tender smile and brimming happiness. Sally was quick to spot things like that, and she was already suspicious.

Sir Warren's death had brought Ruby down to earth with a bump and she grieved for her kind and thoughtful employer. Then she had to think about what she was going to do with herself. Before long she wouldn't have a roof over her head and plans of some sort had to be made without delay.

After the service the lawyer, John Druce, had invited her

into Sir Warren's study, complimenting her on the way she had kept it. Then he had broken the unbelievable tidings that Askwith had left Waterfields to her. It took Ruby's breath away and for a while she couldn't take in what the man was saying. At last she managed to gather her scattered wits together.

"There must be some mistake, sir. He can't have left it to me. I was only his housekeeper."

Druce gave her an approving smile. He liked pretty women, neatly dressed, and industrious. This one wasn't giving herself any airs either. Clearly she thought herself quite unworthy of such a legacy.

"It's true, my dear. Sir Warren had no living relatives, you see, but I'm afraid there's no money to run it. Indeed, a few more pictures and some pieces of plate will have to be sold to meet outstanding debts. Never mind, at least you've got the house. Oh, there's one more thing. Sir Warren left this for you."

When Druce had gone, Ruby went back to the study and broke the seal on the note which the lawyer had handed to her. She recognised Askwith's spidery hand and it made her want to cry again. But sorrow soon turned to mystification. Sir Warren's message to her couldn't have been briefer, consisting of only two words. 'I'm sorry', he had written, not even bothering to sign his name at the bottom of the sheet.

She hadn't the faintest idea what he meant until she started to walk through the house she loved so much. Then she thought she understood. Warren had placed the burden of caring for his precious home on her shoulders, knowing she loved it as much as he had done. His contrition had been brought about by the problems she now faced.

Ruby sat for a while in the window-seat of the master-bedroom. It was obvious that she wouldn't be able to keep Waterfields. She could dip into Albina Pittaway's sovereigns just a little to pay for food, wages and other essentials, but most of the capital had to be reserved.

Even if she used it all, including the value of the rings, it would only mean postponing the inevitable decision for a month or so.

The prospect of sale brought its own anxieties. She remembered only too well what Askwith had said to Lionel Whitcombe when the latter was badgering him to sell. Sir Warren hadn't wanted anyone to have Waterfields, least of all the unspeakable merchant.

When tea-time came her mind was made up. She would give herself two weeks to consider the best way out of her dilemma. With careful marketing she could keep going for that length of time and it would be a marvellous feeling to be the owner of Waterfields if only for so brief a period.

What was going to happen after that she didn't know and for the moment she didn't care. For fourteen whole days the house would be hers, and she was smiling as she went down to the kitchen to tell cook and Janet the news.

* * *

"Left it to his housekeeper?"

Lionel Whitcombe stared at Rowney, his manservant, in disbelief.

"It's true, sir. Got it straight from the horse's mouth, you might say. Janet, the scullerymaid there, is a real gabber. She'd sell her own mother for the price of a hair-ribbon. I've bought a good few tit-bits from that one."

"Christ, and I thought the man was practically a monk."

Rowney was a large, beefy man who had been with the merchant for many years. He was Whitcombe's ears and eyes and sometimes his hands, when there was any dirty work to be done. He was a cynic, always thinking the worst of his fellow man, but this time he shook his head.

"There doesn't seem to have been anything like that. No whisper of scandal, if you see what I mean."

Lionel was even more prone to see bad everywhere and he gave a short laugh.

"Are you seriously telling me that Askwith would leave a place like that to some chit of a girl without getting his money's-worth first?"

"It seems so. He'd no family and Ruby Travers and her mother had lived there for years."

"Well, whatever the reason it's time for me to make my move. This wench knew Askwith didn't want to sell to me. Half Lancashire must have known it by the way he screamed and carried on. Rowney, we've got to find a way of making her accept my offer. Money won't do it. She's got to part with it, of course, because she hasn't got a brass farthing and neither had he. Still, she'd rather sell to anyone in England than me. No, we've got to find a weak spot in her somehow. Even if she had been the old man's bed-warmer, it wouldn't matter much now he's gone. It'll have to be something else."

"Like her uncle being found drunk beside a man stabbed to death and Cuddy Dalton, that's her mother's brother, still holding the knife."

"Her uncle, eh?" Whitcombe turned to look reflectively at Rowney. His servant's information was always reliable. What was more, if a dead man had a part to play in the solution of the problem, Rowney wouldn't cavil at murder. "That sounds promising. Yes, very promising indeed. Pour me a drink, and have one yourself. Then you can tell me all about Miss Ruby Travers' handy relative."

* * *

"I'm afraid it's true, Miss Travers." Whitcome was quite civil for once as he sat in one of the drawing-room chairs which would soon be his. "Your uncle was with some gipsies. He was found as drunk as you please, next to one of 'em. The man had been stabbed and the knife was still in Mr. Dalton's hand. That's so, isn't it, Rowney?"

"Yes, sir, and there were a number of the travelling folk who witnessed it." The lie tripped glibly off the valet's tongue. "They'd come forward, if called, I've no doubt."

"Neither have I." The merchant looked back at Ruby. "The situation's plain enough, as I think you'll agree."

Ruby hadn't sat down. She stood as stiff as starch, glancing from Whitcombe and his servant to Cuddy, who was white and trembling like a leaf.

"I see."

"I'm sure you do." Whitcombe's smile was almost a smirk. "It means the rope, of course."

Cuddy began to moan and struggle in Rowney's hold, gibbering of his innocence, his words falling on deaf ears.

"Unless, sir?"

Ruby was as cold as ice, but she knew the time had come to make good her promise to her mother. Her uncle was in real trouble this time; it wasn't just a bit of pickpocketing. He had killed a man and people had seen him do it. She had given Vinnie an oath, and she knew she had to keep it.

The merchant nodded.

"Yes, I like a quick-witted woman; saves time. You know what I want."

Ruby's eyes moved to Dalton, now down on his knees and slavering like a whipped cur. She had no doubt that Cuddy had committed the crime. He did spend most of his time with the Romanies and he was nearly always drunk. He was also quarrelsome and quite capable of sticking a knife into someone in the heat of an argument.

"I'll think about it."

Whitcombe knew he had won. He could see it in Ruby's face and could afford to give her a few hours grace.

"Until to-morrow morning," he said as he rose to go. "I'll give you a fair price and your uncle will go free. Refuse and he'll swing and you'll have that on your conscience for the rest of your life. And don't get any ideas about spiriting him away. I'm leaving a man on watch to make sure Mr. Cuddy Dalton stays put."

When Ruby and Cuddy went down to the kitchen it was clear that cook and Janet knew all about Whitcombe's visit and his demands. Janet was as nippy on her feet as Elsie had been and even better at listening at key-holes.

Janet wasn't very happy at that moment. It wouldn't take Ruby Travers long to find out who had tittle-tattled to the merchant's servant. Janet disliked the housekeeper most heartily, but she was also in awe of her, and was beginning to wish she'd never opened her mouth. It wouldn't have stopped Mr. Dalton from stabbing a gipsy, but the merchant and Rowney wouldn't have known Cuddy existed but for her.

She drew back into a corner as Cuddy started to plead with Ruby again.

"Girl, don't let them take me. Christ, don't let them! I'm your own flesh and blood. You can't see me dancing in a noose, you know you can't. For your dear, dead ma's sake, you can't let me die."

"Leave my mother out of this conversation."

Ruby was very cool. She had noted the look on Janet's face. It was guilt, plainly written, and it was obvious who had first mentioned Cuddy's name to Whitcombe and his servant. They'd probably kept him under observation since Janet spoke of him, waiting for their tool to put a foot wrong.

She made up her mind quickly. What she had to do made her heart ache, but there was no help for it. First, however, she had to get rid of Cuddy, cook and Janet.

She said shortly:

"No, I won't let you hang, much as you deserve it. To-night you'll leave here. I'll give you money and you can make your way to Liverpool and catch the first ship out. Sally, can you find my uncle some of your old clothes?"

Mrs. Sugarwhite nodded, dazed by the rapid turn of events and unnerved by the proximity of a killer.

"Guess so."

"Then go and get them please. Cuddy, it's Wednesday to-day. Every Wednesday evening, about eight o'clock, Mrs. Sugarwhite goes to see a friend in the village. I'm sure Whitcombe knows this, for it's clear he's been watching us.

His man will think nothing of a woman walking off to Cocker Booth.

"Janet, you'll have to go. I'll give you a week's wages and another sixpence if you'll deliver a note to Mr. Whitcombe for me."

"Anything, Miss Travers." Janet was terrified even now that the housekeeper would find out what she had done. The sooner she got off the better she would like it. Wages and an extra sixpence was a bonus she hadn't expected. "I'll take the note for you."

Ruby gave her a hard stare which made the girl crimson. Then she turned back to her uncle.

"Stop making that noise. I'd better give you a meal, for you won't eat for a while. And make sure you walk slowly across the grounds, as cook would do, or Whitcombe's man will spot you for certain."

Later, when her uncle had gone, Ruby said good-bye to Sally. It was a tearful moment, for the two women were fond of one another, but eventually cook departed wiping her eyes. When she reappeared some five minutes later, Ruby paled.

"What is it? Has Cuddy been caught?"

"No, no, luv, far from it. Thought it would put your mind at ease to know I've just seen the man Whitcombe left to keep an eye on us. He's snoring like a pig and smells like a gin-house. An army could march past him and he'd never notice it. He won't wake till morning; you can count on that."

Ruby gave a deep sigh of relief as Sally waved good-bye again. She had kept her vow to her mother, but now there was real work to be done. She went to the outhouse and got the big can of oil which Askwith had used in the funny crusie lamp a friend had sent him from Scotland. She collected all the candles from the store, together with the rushlights which had been dipped in boiling fat. From the kitchen and larder she took dripping, butter and other fat, smearing it over the furniture and curtains she had cared for so lovingly.

She wished she could take the loom with her, but it was too heavy to move. She stroked it, even touching it with her lips as she bade it farewell. She packed the yarn, shuttles and Albina's wooden box into a hand-cart and left it by the stable door. Then she took a tinder-box and went from room to room.

"You do understand, don't you?" she said to the empty library. "If there was any other way I'd have taken it, but there isn't. I couldn't let my uncle hang, whatever wrong he's done, and I can't sell you to Mr. Whitcombe either. Sir Warren said he'd rather burn you to the ground than let that barbarian have you, and I expect you feel the same."

She stood back, watching the flames begin to take hold. Most of Waterfields was built of timber and by morning it would be nothing but a tangle of charred wood and ashes.

When it was no longer safe to stay, she put on her hat and cloak and walked to the cart. She gave the house one last look, her eyes filled with tears.

"I didn't have you for fourteen days after all, did I? Never mind, even one day was more than I deserved. I'll remember you always, I promise."

Then she turned away and began to push. It would be a long, hard night but she had to be gone before the merchant appeared in the morning to make the offer she had invited from him. She wished she could have seen his face, but that was a luxury she couldn't afford.

She had taken a great risk, but it had been worth it. Lionel Whitcombe would never be master of Waterfields now.

* * *

"That bloody bitch!"

Whitcombe was puce as he surveyed the ruins of the house he had hankered after for so long. Rowney had discovered Grady, the stable-hand charged with the task of keeping the place under surveillance. He was still half-asleep, stinking of spirits, but woke fast enough under a sound thrashing from his master's stout cane.

When Whitcombe had received Ruby's note the night before he had been smugly satisfied. She had agreed to the sale, asking him what he would offer her for the property as it stood. He hadn't had much doubt that his plan would work, for even strong-minded females caved in when a member of their family was in danger. Blood was thicker than water, or so he'd always thought. Now he clenched his jaw as he considered how neatly he had been gulled. She'd even made a mocking jest into the bargain. How much would he pay for the house as it stood. He looked at what was left of it and cursed again.

When he had cooled down a little he stopped to think about Ruby Travers' own loss. She could never have kept Waterfields up and eventually would have had to sell. She would have had money for dresses and hats and all the other nonsenses women put so much store by. Instead, she'd burnt the place rather than run the risk that one day he might acquire it, facing the financial consequences.

It was when he realised how personal her dislike must have been that his own hatred was fanned to white heat. He'd wanted Waterfields so much he could almost taste his longing. It had been a fetish; an object of irrational reverence. Now it was gone but Ruby Travers hadn't, at least, not very far.

"I'll make her pay for this," he said to Rowney later that day. "She won't cheat me like this without suffering for it. I don't care how long it takes, or what I have to do. Before I'm done I'll rub Miss Ruby Travers' nose in this and then I'll break every bone in her body, one by one."

Rowney said nothing. It was always politic to keep silent when Whitcombe was in one of these moods. Words only exacerbated him and the valet had a very strong sense of self-preservation.

"I'm going over to Lady Eyre's." Whitcombe hoisted himself out of his chair, the blood-vessels bulging in his thick neck. "Need something to take my mind off this other business. Got that pearl necklace I bought in London?"

Rowney handed the box to him, his face expressionless. His master wanted Annora Eyre almost as much as he'd wanted Waterfields, and he stood about as much chance of getting her as he had had of getting Sir Warren Askwith's home. It was obvious that the high-born Cyprean was only stringing his master along. Marriage was not on the cards, and even her bedroom was a fortress which Lionel was unlikely to storm successfully. However, if it kept Whitcombe away for a few hours it would be all to the good. If Annora gave him a kiss for the bauble, he'd come back a bit sweeter than when he went.

He bowed his master out of the door and Whitcombe grunted.

"Keep your ear to the ground, Rowney. Anything you can find out about that cow I want to hear it. There's fifty guineas in it for you, if you can help me bring her down."

"I shall do my best, sir, as always." Fifty guineas was like music to Rowney's ears. "I'm sure I'll be able to oblige."

"Hope so." Lionel's eyes glittered with something which even the valet found a bit alarming. "I'm going to ruin her before I'm done, or may God strike me down. I'll finish her, or my name's not Lionel Whitcombe."

* * *

It was nearly dawn when Ruby decided she would have to rest. She was far enough away from Waterfields to avoid being seen by anyone who had noticed the blaze.

She pulled the hand-cart into a clump of trees, steadying it against a thick bush. Then she wrapped her cloak tightly round herself and lay down on the damp grass.

When she awoke she had no idea what the time was, but the sun was high. She hadn't intended to sleep so long, but exhaustion had weakened her body and her will.

She wished there was a stream nearby so that she could wash her hands and face. She hated to be grubby and knew she must look a fright. She was also exceedingly hungry and when she had done her best with her crumpled dress and somewhat battered straw hat, she set off once more, hoping to come upon a hamlet where she could buy food and make herself respectable again. There hadn't been room in the cart for many clothes, but she had grabbed her dark blue serge and grey taminy gowns, together with three clean aprons.

The Earl of Stratton was out for a morning ride. Two days before, on his return from a walk, he had found the two ponderous and ancient horses had mysteriously changed into a pair of exceptionally fine greys. Taxed by his master to explain such a miracle, Wallis claimed to have purchased them very cheaply from a man who was about to leave the country. The earl hadn't believed a word of it, but Wallis stuck firmly to his explanation, and it was good to have a decent mount under one again.

He had done a lot of riding since he had met Ruby Travers. He had wanted to go and see her at Waterfields, but felt that that might have disconcerted her. Instead, he scoured the surrounding lanes and pathways, hoping for a glimpse of her. He knew he was being a fool. He should have put the girl out of his mind and pretended that she didn't exist. There was no future for them, and even one more meeting would bring fresh anguish. All his common-sense and intelligence seemed to have deserted him. Whatever the outcome, and however much it hurt, he wanted to see her again.

He had thought about her constantly. Now and then he remembered Annora, but only in an effort to find a way to rid himself of her. He had had to call on her, of course, because he couldn't afford to alienate her. He found her increasingly tedious and when he was forced to kiss her it was a penance.

He was dreaming about Ruby again when he saw a small figure in the distance pushing a cart. He didn't need to ride closer to know who it was; instinct told him. He dug his heels into the horse's flanks and in a matter of seconds he was looking down at her, his heart beating a good deal faster than he cared to admit.

Her face was smudged with soot, her hair hanging down in untidy wisps. She looked tired and shabby, but her eyes were wholly undefeated.

He dismounted quickly and caught her hand.

"Ruby, what on earth are you doing? That's far too heavy for you to manage."

She gave a wan smile but, like him, she was filled with a sudden flood of happiness.

"You're wrong, sir. I've pushed this wretched thing for miles, although I must admit there were times when I wished it were at the bottom of the sea."

He drew her to the roadside, making her sit on the grass verge.

"What has happened? Tell me what's wrong."

"If you'll promise never to tell a soul about it."

"I won't; you have my oath."

He still held her hand and she dared to close her fingers over his. It was silly to let herself get deeper into a situation which had nothing but torment at the end of it, but she couldn't help it. His strength seemed to flow into her and his touch made her tremble.

He listened to her story, not interrupting her until her voice died away.

"Oh, my dear," he said, wanting to pull her into his arms and comfort her properly. "I am so very sorry. It must have been dreadfully hard to destroy Waterfields. It meant a great deal to you, didn't it?"

"Yes, that's why I had to do it, as I've explained."

"I would like to kill Whitcombe."

She looked up quickly. His voice was harsh and alien to her ears. His eyes were colder than chips of ice, his mouth thinned with the rage in him. It was a side of him Ruby hadn't thought existed, and it frightened her.

"You can't. You mustn't even speak to him of the matter.

You gave your word."

"Yes, I did, and I'll keep it, but I shan't forget what that man did to you." He relaxed, his fury pushed aside. "You're very brave, but what are you going to do now? Dear God, I wish I could help you but I've no money to speak of."

She laughed, feeling better already. Talking to Sebastian and sitting by his side had washed much of her distress away.

"I wouldn't take it even if you had. There's no need for you to be concerned. I'm going to buy a new loom, find a cottage, and start weaving again. Even if you think I'm swollen-headed for saying so, I'm rather expert at it. I've been making fine muslins and cottons for years and they always sell for a good price. Besides, I'm not without means."

She told him about Albina, feeling his hand tighten as if he were afraid she would run away.

"So you see," she finished. "If you are in temporary difficulties I could easily lend you some money. I won't need all of it and there are still the rings to sell. I think they might be valuable."

He had to turn away from the honesty and devotion in her. Annora had made him feel ashamed. Ruby had done much more. She had made him look at himself more minutely than ever. He had led a life of such luxury, cushioned against want and discomfort. He had misused his privileges in a dishonourable manner and, when called to book for it, had done nothing but bewail his lack of funds and modest dwelling. He only had to endure the position for a year. Ruby would have to fight for survival for the rest of her life, but she wasn't complaining as he had done. She was alone in the world, but strong of spirit and so determined. Nothing would ever get her down. He felt lower than a worm as he turned back to face her unspoken question.

"I'll always remember that offer, Ruby, and the girl who made it." For a brief moment he laid his hand on her cheek and it was ecstasy for both of them. "Thank you for letting me see just what I have become."

She didn't understand him, but his soft tone made her

blush and he almost leaned forward to steal a kiss. Then he stopped thinking about himself and his shortcomings and put his mind resolutely to Ruby's problems.

"I'll take you to Wedley on the edge of Will Moor. There's a farmer there and someone told me had had a cottage to let. You shall ride, for you've talked far enough."

Ruby was horrified.

"Sir, I can't let you do that. It would quite ruin your clothes and cover you with dust."

He was wry as he looked down at his long, well-kept fingers.

"The clothes don't matter and it's time these hands did some work. They've been idle for too long. Come along, there you go."

He lifted her into the saddle as if she were a feather, shewing her how to hold the reins. Her cheeks were pinker than ever, for she had felt his body against hers when he had hoisted her up. It was lean and hard and strong and she wanted to become part of it, although she knew she never could.

He gave her a smile as he took hold of the cart's rough handles.

"Come on, Ruby Travers, we're going to get something to eat, buy a loom in the market, and then find you a new home. After that, we'll see. By the way, Mistress Weaver, did you know your hat was on crooked?"

FIVE

When Sebastian and Ruby reached Wedley they found the farmer, Percival Buttle, had already disposed of his empty property. He and his wife, Maud, took an instant liking to their visitors, pressing them to share their midday meal.

Ruby needed no second bidding, and even the earl, normally most finicky about what he ate, tucked in with gusto to pigeon-pie, sweetbreads and a mouth-watering cheesecake.

When Ruby had washed and changed in Mrs. Buttle's bedroom, she and Stratton set off for Thursden where Raymond Worsley, the squire, lived with his family in Coombridge Manor. Percival had assured Stratton that there were two cottages going begging there and it wasn't far off.

Raymond Worsley was a blunt no-nonsense man, who drove his servants and hands hard and had no sympathy for tenants who couldn't pay their dues. His wife was a brown mouse of a woman, his three daughters pale copies of her. They sat in one corner of the room, hardly daring to look up.

But Worsley's son, Jeremy, made Ruby blink. He was very charming with blond curls, blue eyes and a good physique. He was so like her image of Gervase, her phantom friend in Trawley Dale, that it was uncanny. Even his smile was warm and he had a voice to match. Ruby knew that if she had met Jeremy a few years before she would probably have given him her heart. As it was, she had lost that to Sebastian and had nothing for Jeremy but a polite curtsey.

At first the squire wasn't too sure about Ruby. Young, and pretty enough to get herself in trouble. She didn't look to him as if she'd make a good tenant or be regular with her payments. Then he turned to her escort and his doubts subsided. He didn't know what Mr. Clare's relationship with the girl was, nor did he care. Clare was the kind Worsley liked to deal with. Plenty of breeding, every word he spoke carrying authority. A man used to getting his own way, but understanding how the world worked.

While his father was telling the earl about the cottages on the perimeter of his land, Jeremy stared at Ruby in awe. In all his life he had never seen anyone as exquisite as she was and, when she returned his smile, he was lost. He prayed she would take one of the cottages, for then she would be close to the Manor. He could make a point of riding that way every day and the chances of meeting her frequently were rosy.

The squire drove them over to see what he was offering, Jeremy making sure that he wasn't left behind.

As they approached the two gritstone buildings standing on their own, Ruby saw a man bringing pieces of furniture out of one of them. When they grew closer she could see how shabby and ramshackle they were. She could also see the woman at the door, her bony fingers locked tightly together.

"Who is that?" she asked Worsley. "She looks so unhappy. Perhaps she hates to leave here."

"It's Mabel Birtwhistle and she probably isn't too pleased. Couldn't pay her rent so I've turned her out. I'm not a charitable society."

Ruby frowned and Jeremy gave her an apologetic glance. He wanted to explain to his new goddess that his father wasn't really a bad man. Just business-like and not one to forego his rights.

The earl gave Worsley a cold look too. The tenants on his father's country estates often failed to pay on time, if at all, but the marquis had never made anyone homeless in his life. It wasn't that Martin Clare was particularly philanthropic; he simply accepted his responsibilities as a great landowner.

But whereas the earl and Worsley's son remained silent in the face of the squire's action, Ruby did not. As soon as the old landau came to a stop she got out and made for Mabel Birtwhistle.

"I'm Ruby Travers," she said and held out her hand. "I'm hoping to rent one of these cottages from the squire."

Mabel was nearing fifty, flesh pared to a minimum, and a sad, lost look in her eyes.

"Aye, they're both free now. I did me best to keep up t' rent, but in the end I had nowt to give 'im."

She wasn't resentful because Ruby was taking over her home. It wasn't the first time she'd been dispossessed, but it was probably the last. She was a competent spinner, but the local mills could provide yarn quicker and cheaper than that produced on a small mule. The next stop would be the poorhouse, for there was no work to be had. She'd tried the new factories, but they turned her away. They wanted children, and a few experienced men for the more complicated machinery. They didn't want her.

Ruby saw the mule and the solution came to her in a trice.

"I'm a weaver, Miss Birtwhistle, and I've been making muslin for some time now. The house where I worked was ... well ... it caught fire. I'm starting again, once I've got myself settled. I've already bought a loom and it'll be delivered when I send the man my new address. What if I took both places? Part of each could be used for your spinning and my loom. We could have the upper floors for our bedrooms. I need yarn spun for me; you need a place to live. Well, what do you say?"

The look of pathetic relief which filled Mabel's eyes made Ruby want to reach for her handkerchief, but the squire was bent on throwing cold water on the scheme.

"You won't get a return on her; she's finished. She's a bad payer and a slow-coach. You'd do better to go to Potts Mill."

Ruby met Worsley's terse comment head-on.

"Do you weave, sir?"

He scowled, his colour rising.

"Weave? Damn it, of course I don't."

"Then I do not see how you can judge what type of yarn I require. As for Miss Birtwhistle's ability to turn out sufficient for what I want, I've always found that good food makes good workers. Suppose you leave me to worry about my business. I'll give you a year's rent in advance for the two."

As Ruby turned back to give Mabel an encouraging wink, and Jeremy was struck dumb with admiration, the earl said very softly in the squire's ear:

"I would agree, if I were you. I will undertake to see you suffer no financial loss."

Worsley had been about to give an abrupt refusal to Ruby, resenting the wench's sharp tongue and lack of respect. Then he met Stratton's cool, grey eyes and there was something in them which made him nod. He couldn't really understand why he'd caved in so quickly, but the lines at the corners of Mr. Sebastian Clare's mouth meant trouble.

He shrugged.

"Please yourself. If you're fool enough to take a risk, Miss Travers, why should I care?"

"Precisely, Mr. Worsley, and here's your money. Please be good enough to tell your man to put Miss Birtwhistle's possessions back where they belong."

"Listen, young woman, I ..."

"A most excellent suggestion." Stratton didn't raise his voice; he didn't have to. He wasn't his father's son for nothing. "I'm sure you will want to accommodate your new tenant, sir."

When Worsley had ridden off in an extremely ill-humour, Jeremy giving Ruby a regretful shrug, the earl thought it was time he went too. His horse had been brought along with the landau and he mounted up and gave Ruby a smile.

"I can see I'm not wanted. When women start talking about where to put tables and chairs, wise men make themselves scarce. I'll stop at the market and tell them where to send the loom. Is there anything else you need?"

"We shall want food, but perhaps Miss Birtwhistle knows where we can obtain that."

Mabel was dazed by her good fortune. She would sleep in her own hard bed that night, with her own roof over her head. It wouldn't be the workhouse after all and, whatever the squire had said, she would work her fingers off for her new benefactor.

"Aye, village isn't far off. We can get what we need there, that is, Miss, if you've any money left."

"I have and we'll go there straight away. I always do the shopping myself to make sure I'm not cheated."

Sebastian laughed and raised his hand in farewell.

"Good luck to both of you."

"Thank you, sir, you've been kindness itself. I wish I knew how to thank you."

"Perhaps I'll tell you how when next we meet," he said and Ruby blushed a little at the look he gave her. "Until then, Miss Travers."

Ruby watched him until he was out of sight. Then she sighed and turned back to her companion.

"Well, Mabel, for I can't keep calling you Miss Birtwhistle, fetch the baskets, if you will. Bring plenty of 'em, for we shall need to stock up. Besides, I think it's time we got a good, filling meal inside of you."

* * *

"I'm very much afraid that my father was right to send me packing," said Sebastian that night as Wallis laid out his green worsted banyan. "I've learned more about myself in the last few days than in the rest of my life."

"His lordship is a wise man." Wallis knew Stratton hadn't finished and was merely giving him a word or two's encouragement to get the rest of it off his chest. There certainly had been a great change in his master of late, but he doubted whether it was anything to do with the climate of Lancashire. When a man smiled to himself when he thought no one was watching it usually meant a woman was involved. And in the earl's case it certainly wasn't Lady Eyre who had made the difference. "But perhaps there is another cause."

Stratton sighed. He had no secrets from Wallis. His valet horded confidences like a miser did his gold. He could say anything to him and know it would never be repeated.

"I'm very much afraid I've fallen in love."

Wallis didn't shew the slightest flicker of surprise, but then he saw the dejection which crept over the earl like a black cloud covering the sun.

"I see, my lord ... I mean ... sir. Love usually means happiness, but ..."

"... but not for me." Sebastian's voice dropped as if a weight was tied to it. "Ruby, that is her name, wouldn't be acceptable to my father."

"Are you certain of that? His lordship can be very broadminded."

"Not about my marriage and Ruby is a weaver. She was also housekeeper to a man called Warren Askwith. She is more beautiful than all the flowers in a thousand gardens and so full of spirit that she puts me to shame. Yet can you see my father welcoming a servant as my wife?"

Wallis pulled a face. It was worse than he had thought. The marquis might just have been persuaded to accept the daughter of a titled country gentleman. A servant, who was also a weaver, was out of the question.

"Well no, I'm bound to say I can't. Does Lady Eyre know about Miss ...?

"Travers. No, she doesn't." Sebastian turned from the mirror in consternation. "I hadn't given her a thought. If she should find out about Ruby, God knows what she might try to do to her. Annora is excessively jealous and possessive."

"And quite infatuated with your lordship."

"She mustn't find out how much I love Ruby. Whatever happens, we've got to prevent her from knowing that."

"Is Lady Eyre still pressing you to marry her?"

"Constantly."

"If you continue to meet Miss Travers the risk is high."

"I know, I know, but I can't stop seeing her. It's like asking a painter to give away his sight, or a musician to part with his ears. No, I must see her again."

Wallis shook his head. His master was in a bad way, but it wasn't his job to point that out to him. His task was to help the earl to overcome whatever difficulties life had sent to tax him.

"We may have to invent some kind of story," he said as he took Stratton's coat from him. "I must consider the matter."

"What sort of story?"

"I don't know yet, but I'll think of something. You spoke earlier of Squire Worsley's son."

The earl's frown was quick and forbidding. He had noticed Jeremy's interest in Ruby and he hadn't liked it.

"What about him?"

"Well, we could perhaps persuade Lady Eyre to accept that Miss Travers and Mr. Worsley are interested in one another."

"No." Sebastian was very short. "You'll have to think of another idea. I don't care for that one at all."

"As you say, sir, and now may I wish you a good night's sleep?"

"Thank you, but don't ask me to have happy dreams for I doubt if I could manage that." Stratton lay back on the bed and glared at the ceiling. "Oh, hell and damnation! Why couldn't I have been born a weaver too?"

* * *

The next day the earl set out for Chester to see his maternal grandmother, Melesina de Courcy, Marchioness of

Wrensham. His father had been quite right about her. She did have the constitution of an ox and had often been heard to remark that she intended to live to be a hundred.

But Sebastian didn't want his grandmother's fortune; he wanted her advice. It was clear to him that he needed to make some money for himself, for the prospect of existing for the rest of the year on the marquis's allowance was one he didn't relish.

"Serves you right," said the marchioness when she had listened to the whole story. "It was the best thing your father could have done. I might not be gallivanting round London town, but I'm not living on the moon either. I've heard all about your gambling and drinking, your women, and those abominable friends of yours."

"They are no longer my friends, and don't nag. I've come to you for help."

"Money?"

"Yes, but not yours. I want to know how to earn some."

"Makes a change from winning it, I suppose. Not that you often won."

"Damn it, Melly, be serious."

"I am serious. Much more of your fast horses and high stakes and you'd either have broken your neck or bankrupted your father. Oh, all right, all right, I'm finished. So, you want to earn your living, do you?"

"Yes, but I've no idea how to do it. I was brought up to excel in idleness; I've no training for anything but the social graces. How do I market them?"

The marchioness chuckled. She was a small, round woman with a heart-shaped face and a tongue even sharper than the Marquis of Harworth's. She wore a great deal of silks and lace, and outrageous turbans perched on top of her wig. Her late husband had adored her and had tried to make a tame pet of her, but his cause had been doomed from the start.

Melesina was a shrewd, clever woman with a knack of recognising what was important and what wasn't. She had a good head for business and knew to a penny how much she was worth. Her spouse had been a rich man when he had married her. When he died he was wealthier still; Melesina had seen to that.

Her only weakness was her grandson on whom she doted. No one else had ever dared to call her Melly, and no one else could twist her round his little finger like Sebastian did. But she hadn't spoilt him. She had made him see his obligations as the scion of a great House, reprimanding him very tartly when he didn't measure up to her expectations.

She was heartily thankful that Martin had at last put a stop to Sebastian's attempts to kill himself, but now the boy did need a helping hand and she was there to offer it.

"Well now, let me see. I think you can discount your good manners and your looks; neither will get you anywhere except into Annora Eyre's bed."

"Does nothing ever escape you?"

"Not much, and certainly never if it affects you. She's a very silly woman; you should finish with her."

"I can't for the moment. I told you, she's followed me to Lancashire. She's practically on my doorstep and I don't want anyone to know who I am. I'll have to put up with her for the moment, and she mustn't find out about …"

The marchioness's eyes narrowed. She had never seen that look on her grandson's face before, but she knew what was wrong with him. She had seen it on too many faces in her time to mistake it, but she put that matter aside and got down to first essentials.

"Did you know that I own a mill in Lancashire?"

"Good God, no."

"It's called Brindle Mill and it's at Wellsand. Your grandfather bought it because he was fascinated by the new machinery. He soon tired of it, of course, and took to visiting German spas instead. I've been thinking of selling it. I've heard it hasn't got a good name. The manager and his wife leave a lot to be desired and they employ too many small children for my taste."

"You don't usually back away from problems."

"No I don't, but this one's a bit beyond me. I can't go to Wellsand myself and run the place, but you could do it."

Sebastian looked blank.

"Do what?"

"Run the mill. Do pay attention, Stratton, or we shall never get anywhere."

"But I don't know anything about mills or flour either."

"It's not a flour mill, you imbecile. You don't need new machinery to make that. It's a cotton mill; they spin yarn in it."

"Whatever they do in it, I wouldn't be much use, would I?"

"That remains to be seen. If you've got half your father's bottom, you'll do well enough."

"But I ..."

"Be quiet and listen to me. I'll have the place valued and then I'll lend you the money to buy it, at interest, of course."

"You old miser."

"You'll be glad I am, when I'm gone, for everything I've got will go to you. There's one thing I should warn you about. Men don't altogether like these new-fangled factories, as they're called. They think they'll rob them of their livelihoods. There have been some difficulties at Brindle Mill."

"What sort of difficulties?"

"Equipment damaged, that kind of thing. It's not alone in its troubles. If you pay even the slightest heed to what's going on beyond the capital, you'll know there have been many such problems. Some of the factories have been burned down. And there's an unscrupulous creature in the area with mills of his own. He's called Whittle or Whitman, or some such name. He wants all the profits for himself. I suspect he's paying some of my spinners to break up the machines and others to supply him with information which will help him put his competitors out of action. He's done it in other places to my certain knowledge. Also, the foremen and overseers aren't kind to those children; not kind at all."

"I'm not sure whether you're trying to help me, or rescue these luckless infants."

"I'm trying to do both at the same time. Well, what do you say?"

"A Clare in trade?" Sebastian gave a faint laugh. "I'd like to see father's face if he finds out."

"He'll find out. Martin's like me; we don't miss much. But you may be well-established before word filters through to him. Do you accept my offer?"

The earl hesitated a moment or two longer. He didn't really think he'd be a very good mill owner, but he wasn't afraid of trouble and was rather fond of small children. In addition, he needed to increase his income somehow, and Wellsand wasn't far from where Ruby lived.

"Yes thank you, Melly, I will. Heaven knows how I'll get on, but I can only do my best."

"I'll send for my lawyer to-morrow, and you'll be all right as long as you put your mind to it. Now tell me what else is wrong with you."

The earl's smile faded.

"There's nothing else wrong with me. Why should there be?"

"I don't know, that's why I'm asking."

"You're imagining things."

"Liar."

Stratton gave in. There wasn't much point in engaging Melesina in a verbal duel; she always won.

"There is something else."

"I know. Damn it, boy, have you fallen in love?"

The marchioness watched the grey eyes fill with a terrible sorrow and felt a quick stab of fear for Sebastian. This wasn't some idle flirtation, nor did it have anything to do with Annora Eyre.

"Yes I have, but she'll never be mine I'm afraid. When father sent me away he was making my punishment far greater than he knew. I don't think even he would have been so cruel if he'd known what was going to happen. You see, it was here that I met Ruby."

"Ruby, eh?" The old lady stretched out a wrinkled hand and laid it over his. "Pretty name. Well, my dear, you'd better tell me all about her, hadn't you?"

* * *

By June, Molly Caudle and Bertram Corbin had been walking out for three months.

Love had taken the place of friendship very quickly, for they had been attracted to one another from the start. Each needed to grasp any shred of happiness which came their way and they cherished every moment they spent together.

They talked of marriage because they had to have hope to keep them going, but both knew how slender were the chances of such a blissful union. Molly's cottage had only one room, growing more dilapidated with each year that passed. It served as bedroom and kitchen for four growing children, and privacy was unheard of. Furthermore, Timmy had been ill for some months, coughing as his mother had done. He had had to stop work at the mill, for he had no strength for labour. He lay white and still on his thin pile of sacking, eyes sunk into his head.

Recently Gwen had shewn the same symptoms, frail and fretful, no longer crying for food. There was no place there for Bertram and he realised it. His situation was no better. He had an aged mother, querulous and demanding, who lived some ten miles away. Every week, rain or shine, he visited her. He listened to her complaints and grumbles, getting abuse if he ever ventured to point out that she did at least have a roof over her head.

He only earned seventeen shillings a week, but out of that he paid his mother's rent and left her enough for food. By the time he had settled his dues with the woman he lodged with, there was practically nothing left and certainly insufficient to keep a wife. Molly did her best to comfort him when he was down. They both had responsibilities at the moment, she would point out, but in a year or two it would be different.

She knew it wouldn't be, and so did he. It would be a long time before the children were off Molly's hands, and he was convinced that his mother was going to live for ever.

Mostly, they tried to put reality behind them when they went walking. He would put his arm round Molly's waist and she would lean against his shoulder. They would steal a kiss now and then, knowing that sooner or later such exchanges would lead to something more.

Molly hadn't been able to bring herself to tell Bertram about Ham Walkden. She knew she'd have to eventually, but she kept postponing it, afraid she would lose him and with him her will to go on.

On a bright summer's morning they went to Colne Market. They were very quiet because things had grown much worse in the last two weeks. The mules on which Molly worked had been damaged again and she and others had been laid off until they could be repaired. No one knew who was responsible, but the mutterings of the men were getting louder. The industrialists were growing richer and richer, like leeches on their backs, the spinners claimed. It had been better in the old days before the machines had stolen their independence.

Molly owed six weeks rent and the landlord had warned her that she had four days left in which to find it. She hadn't been able to buy any food for two days and had crept out under cover of darkness to steal a few root vegetables from a nearby field.

It broke Bertram's heart because he couldn't do more. He had given her his last few pence and they had come to market to see what they could purchase with them.

"Molly? It is Molly Caudle, isn't it?"

Ruby was shopping with Mabel, her baskets almost full. She had often wondered what had happened to the sad girl who had inherited her grey dress. Sometimes she thought Molly was probably dead, not believing that any human being could endure for long the terrible things fate had visited upon her.

Molly remembered Ruby too. She had never forgotten the beautiful girl and her kind ways. She flushed as she realised how she must appear to Ruby, the latter smart as paint in a blue cotton gown, the low-cut bodice filled in with a large kerchief of finest muslin, and a fetching straw hat.

"Yes it is." Molly shifted from one foot to the other, trying to pretend there weren't holes in her worn-out boots. "I'm glad to sees you, Miss Travers."

"And I you." Ruby had taken in every inch of Molly's apparel and the dark smudges under her eyes. Clearly things hadn't improved and it was time for some more aid to be given. "This is Mabel, a friend of mine. She helps me in my weaving business. She spins and I weave; we are a famous team."

"And this is Mr ... this is Bertram; Bertram Corbin."

"It's a pleasure to make your acquaintance." Ruby summed the young man up in seconds. She liked what she saw and was glad that Molly's life was not entirely empty. "Mabel and I were just going to *The Crooked Staff* to have something to eat. They make most excellent meat pies and their cider is the best for miles around. It would be so nice if you would join us, as my guests, of course."

"We couldn't." Molly pushed the idea away at once. It was charity again and this time she had to stand firm. "You see, we've only just eaten, haven't we Bertram?"

Bertram was ravenous, but he nodded quickly. The very mention of a meat pie made his stomach rumble, but he couldn't let Molly down.

"You're a fibber, Molly, my girl," said Ruby, but her lovely smile and low laugh took all the sting out of the accusation. "Neither of you have had a bite between your lips to-day, I'll be bound. And I'm not taking no for an answer. Come on, follow me and let's have no more of your nonsense."

Trying to stop Ruby once her mind was made up was tantamount to taking on a tidal wave. Before long they were all seated round a rough wooden table, a huge platter of hot pies in front of them. Jugs of cider were produced and Ruby said briskly:

"I want all of those eaten up, mind. I'm not one to waste my money on people with fussy appetites. Here's yours, Mabel. Stick into them, Bertram. Bite them before they bite you."

Half an hour later the dish was cleared, the last drop of cider drunk. Then Ruby demanded a full account of Molly's situation, brushing aside the latter's attempts at subterfuge.

"Well you can stop worrying your head about food and rent," she said when Molly had finished her tale of woe. "I shall lend you five pounds."

"I couldn't! No, no, Miss Travers, I simply couldn't. I don't take …"

"… charity." Ruby laughed again. "I know you don't and I'll not take offence at you calling me Ruby. Now listen to me and don't interrupt. I'm not offering you charity. I'm giving you a loan. I'll charge you interest – one halfpenny on each pound you borrow – so I won't be the loser financially and you can stop going on as if it's being taken out of the poor-box. It'll be just like you going to a bank."

"Are you sure?" Molly didn't know anything about banks and their ways, but the prospect of having some money and keeping her self-respect was a temptation she couldn't resist. "You're absolutely certain, Miss … er … Ruby?"

"Quite certain." Ruby met Molly's anxious gaze unblinkingly. She would never see the money again, with or without interest, but until God was ready to do so, someone had to help people like Molly. "Well, that's settled. Here's your loan. Now you'd better go and spend some of it, hadn't you?"

They parted, Molly weak with relief and full of gratitude; Bertram smiling shyly at the young woman who had saved his love from total despair.

"That girl won't make old bones," observed Mabel as they stopped to buy some soap, candles and a small packet of cinnamon. "She'll go young, you see if she don't."

Ruby and Mabel had got along well from the very first day they had met. They were good friends, but they didn't live in one another's pockets. They took a meal together, by invitation, each respecting the other's right to seclusion. In spite of what the squire had said, Mabel had proved an excellent worker and had an abundance of good sense.

"She's pale, of course, but that's because she's always hungry and the mill is so awful. I don't think she's ill."

"No, at least, no more than any of 'em other poor wretches what have to work in t' mills. I meant I sees something in her. It's just a feeling."

"You and your feelings."

"Laugh at me if you want to." Mabel was used to being teased by Ruby. She didn't mind, because she doted on her. "You think about it, though. You'll come round to seeing I'm right."

And later, when she was alone, Ruby did. Mabel wasn't often wrong about things like that and there had been a light in Molly's eyes which was new. It wasn't caused by hunger, poverty, overwork or pain. It was as if the girl was waiting for something bad to happen. Ruby felt a grue run through her.

"Gracious, woman," she said aloud. "You're what Albina would have called a bluddy fooil. Go and put the kettle on and forget it, or you'll be seeing boggarts before you know it. Molly will be all right because she's in love, and goodness! What a difference being in love can make."

* * *

Molly Caudle wasn't the only one who was 'getten a chap' as Sally Sugarwhite used to say of courting couples.

It hadn't taken the Earl of Stratton long to discover that Ruby's favourite walk was through Owl Wood which lay on the edge of the Forest of Trawden. He hadn't called at her cottage because Mabel Birtwhistle was always about. He thought it might make Ruby uncomfortable, but on reflection he had to admit that he would be the one to feel embarrassment, not Ruby. She seemed to take everything in her stride, always in command of the situation.

But anyone could walk in Owl Wood and very soon he and Ruby met there. He called it a happy chance, but he could see the twinkle in her eyes and had laughed himself. It wasn't easy to fool her.

It became a daily delight, although they didn't speak of their feelings for one another. After they had sat talking he would help her to her feet as if she were a great lady. Ruby thought Vinnie must have felt just the same when Sir Warren opened doors for her. It was nice to be spoilt now and then.

One particular afternoon in June Ruby took her normal route, sensing there was something different about the day. She wasn't sure what made it so but, from the time Sebastian made his bow to her until the time came for them to go, it had been perfect. It was warm, yet there was a slight breeze to cool the cheek and ruffle the hair. Sun broke through the canopy of trees and gilded the rough grass and wild flowers. The birds sang more sweetly than usual; the smells of summer were heady and filled the air with pleasure.

When she took his proffered hand she expected no more than a conventional salutation but, as she rose, her foot caught in a gnarled root. The next moment she was in his arms.

His lips were gentle against hers, but exciting too. He cradled her to him, as if she were a piece of fragile glass, worshipping her with his touch. He made her aware that her body was no longer that of a girl's, demure and unwakened. His embrace turned her into a woman, richly mature and waiting for him to take what he desired.

He let her go reluctantly, his hands still on her shoulders.

"I'm sorry." He was sombre, cursing his own folly. He should never have let it happen, but Ruby had been too near to him for sanity to gain the upper hand. "I shouldn't have done that."

She could see the contrition in him, quick to console.

"Why not? I wanted you to."

"That makes no difference. A man has no right to use a woman like that unless he can take her in marriage. Oh, my lovely, lovely Ruby, do you know how long I have waited to do that? Have you any idea how much I need you?"

She nodded, hardly daring to breathe in case his conscience got the better of him and he fled.

"Yes. It's the same for me."

"I prayed it was, but I can never marry you. I fell in love with you the first time I saw you. Do you remember? You leaned over me and asked if I was hurt."

Her smile was full of tenderness.

"Of course I remember. That was when I knew you would be the only man I could ever love."

"You are my whole world, yet I can't offer for you."

It made it worse that he couldn't explain why. If he could have told her of the marquis's demands on him regarding matrimony it might have been easier for her to understand. As it was, he was aping an ordinary country gentleman and on the face of it there was no reason why he shouldn't ask her to be his wife. He watched her fearfully in case he had hurt or upset her. When she gave the chuckle which always filled him with contentment, the earth seemed to steady under his feet again.

"Of course you can't marry me; do you think I don't know that? You're a gentleman and I'm a weaver and the daughter of a servant. Dearest, it doesn't matter. Don't look like that."

"It matters to me. God designed our meeting and what we share. Men have devised the customs which keep us apart.

"We're not apart. We're here together."

"I shall be leaving Lancashire early next year. After that I shall never see you again."

It was a body blow, but Ruby didn't flinch. She had to be strong, for he needed help just as he had done on that first day.

"Then we'll have to make the most of our time, won't we? Each kiss must be a perfect one; every time you hold me I shall treasure the feel of you."

He was frowning again, stumbling over a fresh difficulty.

"That is all there can be, you realise that? I can't ... I won't ... There will just be kisses and the bliss of being with you; nothing else. You can't belong to me in the way I would wish. Will it be enough?"

It was a second jolt. Ruby had been carefully raised, but all her mother's teaching meant nothing now. She had been prepared to forget modesty and morals, for only Sebastian was important, and she wanted their union to be complete. But she gave no indication of her melancholy, for he was in torment waiting for her reaction. Disappointment and a curious sense of loss had to be put aside and, after all, he cared enough about her not to make her a wanton.

She smiled at him as Vinnie had smiled at her when she had gone running to her mother with a grazed knee.

"It will be plenty for me. Just seeing you would have been enough."

"You're so brave. You make a coward of me."

"You could never be that."

"You may change your mind when I have to go. Ruby, I don't know how I'm going to say good-bye to you. It will be like dying, and I don't want to die alone."

"You won't have to; I shall be there."

He took her face between his hands, studying the steady courage in her eyes, wondering if she noticed the tears behind his own.

"Thank you," he said at last and let his hands drop to his sides. "I didn't deserve to meet you, nor do I merit your love. You are everything to me and always will be. Whatever happens during the rest of my days, you will be with me. Even when many years have gone by, I shall see you as you are to-day. You won't grow old to me. You will stay young and beautiful and gallant, resting in my heart. Oh, my darling, darling girl."

They came together again in desperation. Ruby had vowed to herself that she wouldn't cry and make his grief harder for him to bear, but it wasn't easy. Drop of moisture pricked behind her closed lids, demanding to be set free to mourn, but she held them back with fierce resolution.

They clasped hands as they walked back the way they had come, not speaking. Words wouldn't serve them now and there was always the danger of a quaver in the voice which would betray them. When they reached the spot where the earl's horse was tethered it was Ruby who took the lead.

"To-morrow? I thought I might make some ratafia cakes and bring a bottle of cider. We could have a picnic, couldn't we? Or would you prefer almond tarts and wine?"

He held her hand against his cheek, still unable to find a smile for her.

"Just come yourself, beloved. The rest is of no consequence."

Then he turned away, walking rapidly as if a devil was snapping at his heels. Ruby watched him mount up and ride off and then at last her brittle control broke into smithereens.

Sebastian wouldn't be the only one to die a little when the time came for them to part. Her life would be over, too, and she buried her face in her hands and sobbed as if her heart would break.

SIX

"You're going into trade? In one of those awful mills? Sebastian, have you lost your wits?"

"No, my income. You forget, Annora, I'm practically a pauper. I've got to do something to make money until I'm out of father's bad books. My grandmother's proposal is the only way I can see out of the mess."

Lady Eyre was outraged. She had thought the earl was coming round to seeing things her way. Instead, he had embarked upon a hare-brained scheme which could ruin him socially if news leaked out of his activities.

"But what will the marquis say?"

"I hope he won't find out, but if he does he'll have to put up with it. After all, it's because of him I'm placed in this position."

Her azure eyes snapped with vexation.

"You know quite well there's an alternative."

Stratton tried not to think of Ruby as he looked at the irate Annora. She wore a confection of pink and white, her blonde hair elaborately dressed. She was as artificial as Ruby was natural, but he still dared not alienate her. It was a miracle that word of Ruby's existence hadn't reached her yet. He wasn't sure how long his luck would hold and he had to pretend he was still interested in her way out of the catastrophe.

"Yes, my dear, I know and please don't think I'm insensible to the honour you pay me." The words almost choked him, but he continued gamely. "I'd like to try this first. I wouldn't want to come to you a failure. Give me a chance to see what I can do with this factory. If time proves I'm no good at such things, as very likely it will, then we'll talk about your suggestion again."

Annora's foot was tapping impatiently. She didn't want to wait months for Stratton. Indeed, she didn't want to wait for him at all. He filled her with hot desire and she wanted to pull him upstairs to her bed without further delay. Unfortunately, that would not be at all *comme il faut* and such behaviour might scare him away for good.

She contemplated the possibility of informing the marquis, but soon dismissed that idea. If Sebastian should find out what had done it would all be over between them.

"How long am I expected to stay here twiddling my thumbs?" she demanded, seeing there was no choice but to exercise her patience. "I do hope you're not trifling with me, my lord."

He had drifted off again, thinking of Ruby's kiss, but her acid tone put paid to his dreaming.

"No, no, of course I'm not. Let's say three months. Then we'll see."

Annora could tell it was the best she was going to get out of him, her lips tight with anger.

"Very well, if you insist on behaving so absurdly. Three months, but not a day longer, and I shall expect you to dine with me to-morrow. Do you hear me, Sebastian?"

"I always hear you, my dear," he said with some feeling. "It's rather difficult not to."

She was still furious when Lionel Whitcombe was announced. He had become even more ardent since she had arrived in Lancashire, bombarding her with jewels and other trifles in an attempt to worm his way into her affections.

She gave the merchant a brief nod as he made his bow. Lionel never blustered in Lady Eyre's presence. He was the supplicant, fawning and servile, wanting her plump, luscious body with such intensity that he always sweated profusely whenever he was near her.

She accepted his latest offering, a diamond necklace of considerable worth, the warmth of her thanks carefully calculated. She didn't want him to get above himself, but the stones must have cost a great deal and he deserved some reward.

Then she got down to business, telling Whitcombe of the earl's plan, and bidding him to keep the information to himself. He was amazed that the marquis's son should take it into his head to dabble in such an enterprise, but Annora gave him no time to ponder on the bizarre decision.

"He says if the mill fails he will consider marrying me. That's good enough, for he'll need my fortune. His father will keep him on a tight rein from now on and Sebastian has expensive tastes. He knows he'll have to trim his sails, even after the marquis permits him to return home. He'd rather wed me and go on spending. I want you to make sure the mill does fail."

Lionel drank his fill of her, watching her fasten the necklace round her milk-white throat.

"Why should I dig my own grave?" he asked, mopping his brow. He'd never known a woman do things to him as Annora Eyre did. "I want to marry you myself."

She turned from the mirror and gave him a derisive glance.

"Why should you help? Because you know perfectly well I'd never consent to be your wife; you're a peasant."

It felt as if she were whipping him, but he was enjoying the sensation.

"If you were a man I'd knock you down for saying that."

"If I were a man you wouldn't want to sleep with me."

"What do I get out of this, except ridding myself of some competition?"

Annora's lips parted, her tongue moistening them until they were red and glistening like cherries washed by rain. Whitcombe tugged at his stock, suddenly far too tight for comfort.

"If you'll do this for me, I'll become your mistress. Only

for a while, of course, and Stratton must never find out or he'd be finished with me for good. And don't forget; you're never to let anyone know who he really is."

"How do I know you'll keep your word? What's to stop you crying off after I've shut his lordship's factory down for him?"

"You could do it, then, without Sebastian knowing either of us was involved?"

"Easy as pie. I've done it times enough and that sort of thing's going on all over. The workers are making trouble everywhere. This won't look any different, but …"

He broke off, his jaw slackening. Lady Eyre had removed the buffon from her shoulders, the low-cut gown revealing the magnificence of her full, creamy breasts. His eyes glazed as she took a deep breath and allowed him a tantalizing glimpse of the rosy nipples.

"Come upstairs." Her scorn for the brutish financier was increasing. He was putty in her hands and she had no time for men like that. She wanted a master and she was pretty sure that she'd find one in Stratton. He might be at a low ebb where money was concerned, but she'd heard tales about him from other women which had made her perspire almost as freely as Whitcombe. She would have to grit her teeth whilst the merchant slobbered all over her and took what he wanted, but he would be her slave for life. If she were ever to become the Countess of Stratton, Sebastian's venture must be reduced to rubble. Lionel Whitcombe knew how to achieve that and she had to meet his bill. "Well, sir? Is it a bargain?"

He followed her upstairs, feeling as if he'd drunk a barrel of cognac. He had never expected his fantasies to be transformed into realities and he blessed the circumstances which made Annora require his services. But for that, he knew he'd never have seen the inside of her bedroom.

When she was naked he tried to grab her, but she held up one hand.

"I have your solemn promise?"

"Anything. Jesus, you're beautiful."

"Of course." Her eyes were as cold and unfeeling as pieces of glass. Undressed, Whitcombe looked more like a fat pig than ever, but even pigs had their uses. "Otherwise you wouldn't want me. Well, this is your first payment. There's the bed; let's get on with it, shall we?"

* * *

On the same day that Lionel Whitcombe got his heart's desire, Molly Caudle and Bertram Corbin were walking through the Forest at Rossendale.

At mid-day they shared a pot of crowdie which he had begged from his landlady. It consisted of oat-meal over which boiling water had been poured. It had long since grown cold and was far from appetizing. Molly's contribution was some pieces of hard oaten cake. They weren't even aware of what they were eating. They were together and that was what mattered.

They had always shewn one another affection. Molly blushed when Bertram kissed her and he liked to feel her thin arm about his waist. Neither had ventured further until that hot July day.

Molly stretched out under the trees, grateful for the shade. Her dress was torn again, the skirt parting to shew her thigh. Bertram looked at it for a long time; then his gaze travelled upwards.

When he caught hold of her she cried out in protest, but he wouldn't listen at first. She felt his lips against her flesh, her heart pumping violently. She wanted him as eagerly as he wanted her, but she had to make a confession first.

"Wait! Bertram, wait. There's summat I've got to tell you."

At first she thought he wouldn't stop to listen, but in the end he sighed and let her go.

"Just like a woman to want to chatter at a time like this. Put me right off, you will."

"That's what I'm afraid of."

"Oh?" He could see she was serious and near to tears. "Here, lass, what's to do? Maybe I shouldn't have done that, seeing we can't be man and wife for years yet. I didn't mean to upset you."

"No, it's not that. I told you; it's summat you have to know."

He nodded.

"Go on then. Get it off your chest if it'll make you feel better."

"It won't make you feel better. Likely as not you'll get up and go and never want to see me no more."

"Have to be something pretty dreadful for that to happen, Moll."

"It is ... was dreadful."

He gave her a playful squeeze.

"Don't reckon you could do anything that bad."

She met his eyes, praying he would understand. She didn't think he would, for men were funny like that. Decent men like Corbin didn't want someone else's leavings.

She told him plainly, and without trying to justify herself, what had happened in the storeroom at Brindle Mill.

"And it weren't the last time neither. I had to stop Walkden from hitting Timmy, but I know it's no excuse."

He pulled her closer to him, his heart aching for her.

"I understand," he said gently. "I know what you girls go through in that bluddy mill. Seen it often enough with my own eyes and it weren't as though you did it for extra food or to save yourself from a beating. It were for Timmy. Poor little bastard's half-dead because of what men like Walkden did to him. Anyone 'ud have done the same if they cared about their kin as you do."

"But I'm a whore, Bertram, a whore! I'm not whole or clean or decent, and I do love you so much."

She sobbed in his arms and he whisperd tender words in her ear until she was quiet again.

"Don't make a jot of difference to me," he said when

Molly lay back on the grass again. "I want you just like I did ten minutes ago."

"You mean it?" Her eyes lit with hope. "You honestly mean it?"

"Well, seeing you don't want to take my word for it, how about me shewing you some other way?" he drew the dress from her shoulders and she gave a deep sigh. It felt so different from that first time when Ham had laid hands on her. "There, that weren't so bad, were it?"

"No, it were wonderful. Oh, Bertram, if you means it, let's do it, eh?"

"No way stopping me now." He grinned as he bent to kiss her. "You thought Ham Walkden had made a fallen woman out of you. Now you just see what I can do, my girl. Oh Moll, whatever made us wait so long?"

* * *

Two weeks after Sebastian had told her he loved her, but that their time together would be short, Ruby decided it was time she took him in hand.

In the interval her business prospects had taken a sharp upward turn. A good-sized and regular order for finest muslin had been secured and she was looking for larger premises to carry out the work. She had even taken on two more girls, bought another loom and a rather ancient wooden mule. It made her feel like a capitalist and the two cottages were bursting at the seams with all the activity going on inside them.

But her walks with Sebastian hadn't been nearly so satisfactory. He shewed a marked tendency to fall into silences, and to sit an unnecessary distance away from her when they did talk. What was worse, he hadn't put a hand on her for days, never mind about giving her a kiss.

She knew he had a lot on his mind, for he had told her of his intention to acquire a mill. He hadn't said a lot about it and she hadn't pried. Perhaps later he might want to discus his investment; she would be there to listen when he was ready.

She was sure it was something quite different which troubled him and, not being one to allow awkward situations to continue if there was a remedy, she sat herself down on a tree trunk and said firmly:

"Don't you think it's time we talked about this? The days are slipping by and they'll soon turn into weeks and months. Then you'll be gone and we shall have wasted the most important part of our lives."

He was digging a hole in the ground with the tip of his riding-whip, affecting ignorance.

"I don't understand. Discuss what?"

"Sebastian! You know well enough what I'm talking about."

He grimaced. It was no good playing that game with Ruby, but he was still very much on edge.

"You mean because I haven't ... well ... we didn't ..."

"You've been treating me like your maiden aunt, and what about those special kisses I wanted? You don't touch me, except to help me up. You're afraid, aren't you?"

He gave up. It was useless to hold the truth back any longer.

"Of myself, yes. Ruby, I adore you. Just the sight of you makes a madman of me. I'm frightened that if I kissed you again as I did that day I wouldn't be able to stop there. I swore I wouldn't harm you and I mean to keep my word."

She understood him so well, as if she had the key to the secret places of his mind.

"What about me? It's all very fine for you, but I don't like it this way."

"I've told you; I don't trust myself."

It was time to take the pain away and she said softly:

"You old silly. Haven't you ever heard of comfort kisses?"

He raised his head and saw the wealth of love and compassion in her. It was as if she were lifting a heavy burden from him, taking it on her own shoulders.

"No, I don't think so. What are they?"

"Just what they sound like. They're the sort of kiss you give someone to make them feel better and to shew that to care, but without getting into ... well ... other things. Now, courting kisses aren't the same. That's when a boy and girl make up their minds to wed. I wouldn't recommend that sort for us, but the other kind are quite safe."

The earl went on digging his hole for a minute or two, Ruby's hands locked together under her apron where he couldn't see them. She wasn't sure whether she'd succeeded or not, but she'd soon find out.

"No, you're right. They would be very risky in the circumstances. On the other hand ..."

"... one comfort kiss is worth a dozen doctor's potions, or so Albina told me. You remember that I explained about Mrs. Pittaway?"

"I never forget anything you say." He was still reserved because he wanted to seize her, tear every stitch from her body, and make wild, passionate love to her. "She left you a loom, some money, and three rings. You offered to lend me some of your legacy."

"That was nothing." She got up and went to sit beside him. He stiffened, sensing danger, and still not at all sure about giving her a kiss, whatever kind it was. When she slipped her arm through his, it was all he could do not to cut and run.

She turned his face to hers, her fingers like the wings of a butterfly on his cheek. Then she put her arms round his neck, drawing his head down and kissing him gently and without a trace of desire.

It was a most agreeable sensation. Suddenly Sebastian's arm was round her and not a shred of his former doubt remained. She'd been right, as usual. Comfort kisses weren't like making love at all. They made him light-hearted and secure, even pushing into the background of his mind the thought that he was going to lose her.

"I've never met a woman like you before," he said with a

sigh. "You must be a witch, for you can achieve the impossible. I feel much better, don't you?"

"I'm as happy as a lark and I'm not a witch. I just see things straighter than you, that's all."

"My sweet, practical, marvellous Ruby. What should I do if you weren't so sensible?"

"Moon and mope over things that can't be mended."

She had laid her head against his chest, glad that he couldn't see her expression. In spite of her bracing words she had never been unhappier or less in control of things. Comfort kisses were all right, but courting kisses were what she wanted. When it was time to go she was herself again.

"Now we've solved the problem, could we practise a bit?" Sebastian asked hopefully. "Just to make sure I'm really doing it properly."

"I don't see why not. Wouldn't do for you to get them mixed up, would it?"

"Quite fatal."

Just for a second their eyes met and each saw the reflection of their own suffering. Games didn't make tragedy go away. They just masked it a bit so one could go on living. Ruby put her hands in his, smiling at him as if they were going to be together for the rest of time.

"Off we go then, Mr. Sebastian Clare. Here's your second lesson for to-day."

His fingers tightened over hers as he bent his head, worshipping her with his own smile.

"And here, Miss Ruby Travers, is your second comfort kiss. The third will probably be better still, the fourth quite perfect. Oh, my dearest one; thank you for shewing me the way out of hell."

* * *

"Madam, you must be insane. If you're not, then I must assume you did it simply to make mischief."

The Marquis of Harworth was furious as he paced

Melesina de Courcy's drawing-room. It was a scorching August day and his lordship had come hot-foot from London, pausing only to deposit his luggage at *The White Falcon Inn*, then driving recklessly to Linacre Lodge on the outskirts of Chester.

Before leaving town his wrath had fallen upon Edington. The agent appointed by the lawyer, one William Grace, had only discovered the earl's proposed purchase of the mill two days before. The marquis had told Edington just what he thought about his handling of the situation, adding a pithy post-script about the antecedents of the unfortunate Grace.

The Marchioness of Wrensham sat by an open window, wearing a stylish gown of pomona green, and totally unmoved by her irate visitor. She had been expecting her son-in-law for some time, wondering why it was taking him so long to find out about the scheme. His ill-humour was not surprising, but she was too old to worry about men's tantrums.

"My dear Harworth, for heavens sake calm yourself. And don't stamp about on my carpet. It came from Persia and it's very valuable."

"To hell with your carpet! What in God's name made you encourage Stratton to embark upon so ill-advised a venture?"

"He came to me and sought my advice as to how he could make a living. I wanted to get rid of the mill so I suggested he bought it."

"How could he buy it?" Harworth was diverted for a second. "He hasn't any money."

"I lent it to him."

"At interest, no doubt."

"Naturally." She was blandness itself. "I'm a business woman, you know that."

"Business woman! Christ, Melesina, my son in trade? Even now I can hardly credit that you would sit by and allow this to happen, never mind being instrumental in bringing about such a crass piece of folly."

"Don't be a dolt, Martin. You sent him away practically penniless. What did you expect him to do?"

"Learn his lesson?"

She jeered at him.

"On fourpence a week? Did you really think he'd knuckle down under your sentence? He's your son. You should have been prepared for him to fight back."

"Fighting back is one thing. Becoming a tradesman is quite another matter."

She took a sip of Madeira and cackled.

"Been all right if he'd taken a run at you with a rapier, I suppose? Don't be such an arrant snob. You're only out of countenance because he's been bright enough to pay you back in a way which has got right under your skin."

"With your help."

"Better mine than the money-lenders," she retorted. "Sit down and have some more brandy and leave Stratton alone. Let's see what he's made of. You took your time discovering what was afoot. How did you learn about it in the end?"

He told her of the surveillance on his heir and Melesina sniggered again.

"No wonder you're in such a pet. Your man must be blind, deaf and dumb."

The marquis ignored the gibe, but he did sit down and take a much-needed drink.

"I think I should call him home at once."

"Doubt if he'd go back to London now. The legal work's almost done and he'll take over in September. I think he's looking forward to it."

Again Harworth let the comment pass. He had another matter nagging at him which was of more importance.

"William Grace may be slow but he's thorough. He's told Edington about a girl called Ruby Travers. It seems Sebastian has been seen with her on a number of occasions. Do you know her?"

For the first time the marchioness wasn't amused. She didn't care a jot about Harworth finding out about the mill, but she had hoped he'd never hear about the woman Sebastian loved.

"How could I?" She was waspish, trying not to look guilty. "If she's in Lancashire, as I assume she is, and I'm here in Chester it's not likely we'd meet, is it?"

"Don't prevaricate. You know perfectly well what I mean. Did Stratton mention her to you?"

"If he had, it would be none of your business."

The marquis's temper had been at boiling point for forty-eight hours but suddenly it evaporated.

"You know it has to be my business," he said quietly. "Don't fight me on this."

Melesina raised her hands helplessly. He was right, of course, but she wasn't going to let her grandson down if she could help it.

"It was a confidence."

"And I will keep it so. Anyway, you didn't tell me about her; Grace did. I take it it isn't serious. I understand she's a weaver. I suppose Sebastian couldn't afford his normal, high-priced bed-fellows, so he turned to this wench instead for amusement."

When the marchioness remained silent, Harworth said sharply:

"She is a harlot, isn't she?"

The old lady kept him waiting a little longer and when she did answer him it was with another question.

"Martin, do you remember the day you met Isabella? Can you recall it after so long?"

The marquis looked down at the heavy gold signet ring he wore. His dead wife had given it to him when they had married and he had never taken it off since. He said slowly:

"I can recall the day, the time, the place, and precisely what she was wearing, even down to her yellow kid slippers. Why did you ask that?"

"Because it is the same for Sebastian. He loves this girl just as much as you loved my daughter."

"But she's a common villager."

Melesina gave him a quizzical smile.

"Look at me, Harworth, and tell me what you would have done if Isabella had woven cloth for a living instead of being the offspring of a nobleman."

The pause was longer that time.

"I'm not sure," he replied eventually. "I would have loved her just the same, of course, but ..."

"And you'd have married her. All your talk about preserving the name of your House! The noble women whom men had to marry, however plain the wretches were, just to keep the blood-like pure. It's all poppycock and would have gone straight out of the window, and you know it."

"But it didn't happen that way."

"No, but it's happening now, to your son. Before you make a final decision do one thing for me. I don't often seek favours, do I?"

He shook his head.

"No, but that's because you're as stubborn as a mule and a damned sight too independent. All right, what do you want of me?"

"Don't rely upon this man Grace to tell you about Ruby. Go and find out about her for yourself."

"How can I possibly do that?"

"Good heavens, man, use your imagination if you've got any. Discover where she lived and who her parents were. Talk to the people who knew her. Find out what sort of woman she is and try to see her without her seeing you."

The marquis was studying his ring again, a shadow in his eyes.

"I'll consider it, but you realise that I can give no promises whoever makes the enquiries."

"I suppose I'll have to make do with that. At least keep an open mind for the time being and, my dear, don't hurt the boy more than you have to if, in the end, there's no hope for him."

"I'll do everything I can to ease his pain. At least I can give you my word on that. You forget, I love him too."

"Then give him a chance." The marchioness thought she could see the merest chink in Harworth's armour and it was worth working on. "What difference is it going to make to the grand scheme of things if just one Clare out of all those who've gone before, and those who will come after, marries a workwoman instead of a duchess?"

"I've told you, I can't promise."

"Since you haven't replied to my question I'll do it for you. It wouldn't make a ha'porth of difference and in your heart you know it. Now go away, do, you've given me a headache and I want to take a nap."

The marquis left the house and made his way to the phaeton. He decided to go back to town that night, for he had a lot of thinking to do before anyone started asking questions about the Travers girl. Stratton would have his hands full for the time being if he were to become the owner of a mill in the following month. In addition, there had been nothing in the agent's reports to indicate that Sebastian was making any rash or precipitant moves regarding matrimony.

Harworth hadn't admitted to Melesina the truth about his own love, but he couldn't leave Isabella in any doubt. Although she'd left him many years ago, he was sure she could still read his heart as easily as she had one when she was alive. Nevertheless, it was as well to reassure her.

"Oh yes, Belle," he said softly, almost seeing her smile and sensing the light perfume which she'd used. "I would have made you my wife, no matter what. If you'd been a weaver, a pot-house wench, or even a nightingale, it would have made no odds. I'd have married you anyway. Your mother knew that, blast her. I loved you and that was the only thing which ever mattered to me."

He took the reins between his hands, bowling down the road which led to the centre of Chester and *The White Falcon*.

The marchioness had been right about another matter as well. When the time came, he couldn't leave William Grace to investigate the history of Miss Ruby Travers. That was something he was going to have to do for himself.

SEVEN

It was not only the Earl of Stratton who had made a point of seeing Ruby regularly. From the day she had moved into his father's cottages, Jeremy Worsley had been a constant visitor.

Ruby had grown fond of him and, in a way, it was a relief to be with a personable young man who didn't wrench one's heart to pieces. She still found it strange that he resembled so markedly her childhood sweetheart. Gervase had been a dream, but Jeremy was flesh and blood, good-humoured, and easy to talk to.

At first she had found his obvious admiration flattering. When the compliments became more personal and the light in his eyes changed to something she recognised all too well, she knew that eventually she would have to put him straight.

Matters came to a head one day early in September. Worsley had coaxed her out of the stuffy cottage to stroll across an adjoining meadow. She noticed he chose the opposite direction to Coombridge Manor and wasn't surprised. Squire Worsley didn't like her. They had struck sparks off one another at their first meeting and he certainly wouldn't want his only son to be seen in the company of a humble weaver.

It was late in the afternoon, the sun beginning to dip in the west. In the nearby fields the harvest was already in. All that was left of Nature's bounty was a short golden stubble and a bundle of wheat which someone had forgotten to take to the granary.

"I must talk to you, Ruby," said Jeremy after they'd been

walking for a while. "It's important."

She knew what he was going to say and tried to stop him.

"What a coincidence. I was going to talk to you, too, about larger premises for my work. The cottages aren't big enough what with extra hands and this new order."

"Don't." For once he wasn't smiling. "You know what's on my mind and you're just trying to put me off."

Ruby stopped and turned to him.

"Yes I am, but it's for your own sake."

"If you're really thinking about me, then listen. I love you and I want you to be my wife."

"I can't see your father taking kindly to that idea."

"He isn't being asked to marry you."

"He'll raise enough objections to drown the pair of us."

"Let him. My dear, I need you so very much."

She felt genuine sorrow for him as she searched his troubled face. There was no doubt that he meant what he said and she hated to hurt him. Still, the injury would be greater if she didn't make things plain at once.

"I'm grateful, Jeremy, truly I am."

"I'm not asking for gratitude."

He knew his case was hopeless. He'd seen it all along, but his passion for the girl with the dark, glowing eyes and lovely smile made him determined not to give up without a fight. His father would raise Cain, but that was of no consequences. If Ruby would only give him a chance he would have taken on battalions for her.

"It's all I've got to give you." She tried to make it as easy on him as she could. "Any woman would be proud to have the love of a man like you, but I can't return it. I'm fond of you, you know that, but there's no more."

He felt chilled, as if death had moved the hands of a clock to point to the hour of his going. He wanted to shout to her that she'd been seen with Sebastian Clare, but that would only make her walk away from him and destroy what little happiness he had. When he was sure his voice was steady enough he said quietly:

"I shan't give up all hope. One day you might change your mind."

"I won't and don't hanker for things you can never have. That's like stabbing yourself with a knife."

She said it with such a depth of feeling that his own heartbreak was forgotten for the moment. If she'd fallen in love with Clare he was sorry for her. He didn't know much about the handsome stranger who had suddenly appeared in their midst, but he recognized the man's quality and knew Clare would never marry beneath him.

If he, Jeremy, were patient and didn't press Ruby, she might turn to him in spite of what she'd said. When Clare had gone, and the latter wasn't the type to stay in the North of England for very long, Ruby would be alone and needing someone. His best chance was to wait and see what the future brought.

"All right, we'll leave it for now. Tell me about the new place you've looking for. Perhaps I can help."

"I don't want to impose on you, especially after what I've just said."

His laugh was as easy and natural as ever.

"Oh come on, Ruby, we're good friends if nothing else. Stop being a ninny and tell me what you want. You can use me as much as you like and I shall enjoy it."

She breathed a sigh of relief. He had taken her rejection well and hadn't withdrawn his companionship. She was glad of that, for she would have missed it.

"Very well, use you I will. Now, what I require is something like a large barn which will take two looms, mules, bales of material and four busy women."

"I know the very thing. If I tell you where it is, will you invite me home to tea?"

"Blackmailer."

"Just an opportunist."

"I give in. May we see it now? Is it far away?"

"No, it couldn't be closer. As to whether I take you there this minute depends on what's for tea."

"Toast, with fresh butter and damson jam; fruit scones, and gingerbread."

"We shall go to Corbel's Farm this very instant."

"Why, that's just over there, quite close to Coombridge Manor. And you're a pig."

"I know," he returned shamelessly, "but no one makes gingerbread as well as you do. Thank you, Ruby."

She knew he wasn't expressing gratitude for a slice of cake. In a way it was rather like the help she'd given Sebastian. She had shewn the latter how to make the best of things as they were, without the agony of severed ties. Now she had given Jeremy the same chance and he had taken it. Neither of the solutions were satisfactory. They were just nailed roughly together and could split asunder at any time, for they hadn't been made to last. She thrust her doubts and regrets aside, for they were only weakening.

"Very well," she said. "Shew me this wonderful barn of yours, for until I've seen it you'll not get gingerbread or anything else come to that."

He caught her hand and began to run, Ruby's hat falling off, her hair tumbling to her shoulders as the stiff breeze caught it.

"Oh you wretch!" she cried, joining in his laughter. "Look what a scarecrow you've made of me. I'll pay you out for this, Jeremy Worsley, just you see if I don't."

* * *

"Corbel's old barn, eh?" Lionel Whitcombe was rubbing his chin. "When's she moving in?"

"Next week, I'm told."

"Good. We'll let her get settled in nice and snug and then we'll give her a dose of her own medicine. You've done well, Rowney, very well."

"I always aim to please, sir."

"So you do. Find a few reliable men who can keep a still tongue in their heads. After it's over, if all's gone well, you'll have the fifty guineas I promised you."

"So generous, sir."

"Aye, that I am to those who serve or please me. You serve; Lady Annora pleases. I'm just off to see her again. Got her these. What d'you think of 'em? Reckon she'll like them?"

The valet inspected the emerald earrings with the care they deserved. Going right overboard for Lady Eyre, were the master. Been much better-tempered of late as well. Almost as though he'd stormed the ramparts after all.

"They're perfection. Any woman would give her soul for them."

Whitcombe gave a satisfied chuckle. He had no doubt his mistress would be delighted with them, for she had a weakness for emeralds. It felt good to think of her in those terms. She'd said he could be her lover for just a while, until he'd closed down Sebastian Clare's mill, but he'd put no time limit on his undertaking and it could be strung out for quite a while.

"Maybe, but it's not their souls you want to go for, Rowney, it's their bodies. Take my advice, leave their souls to their Maker; you take what's left."

* * *

By the end of September Ruby and her helpers were well-established in their new premises. The place was a hive of industry and even more orders had been received. Agnes Micklewhite and Mary Skegg had proved good and reliable workers, even staying late when customers clamoured for quick delivery.

The barn was conveniently close to Ruby's cottage as well as to Coombridge Manor. Jeremy Worsley called each day, just to make sure that all was well. Ruby and Sebastian continued to meet in Owl Wood, neither letting the other know that they were watching the sands of time run out.

"Well, that's enough for one day," said Ruby at six-thirty

one Friday evening. "We've got through a lot this afternoon and it's time you took your wages and got yourselves home."

"I just want to finish off this piece, Miss Travers," Mary let the treadles rest for a moment or two, inspecting her handiwork. "Wouldn't like to leave it like this. I've only got an inch or so to do. You go; I'll be all right by myself."

Ruby was doubtful.

"There's the locking up to do."

"I can see to that and I'll drop the keys at your cottage on me way t' village. I'll do it proper."

Ruby preferred to see to the securing of the doors herself, but she didn't want Mary to get the idea that she wasn't trusted. Besides, when a girl was conscientious enough to want to complete the job in hand, it wasn't wise to discourage her.

"All right, but don't make it too late, mind. Here are the keys; see everything's ship-shape, won't you?"

Ruby and Mabel had supper together that night. They usually shared the meal on a Friday, taking it in turns to prepare the food. Mabel carved the boiled leg of beef, done to a turn in its stock of cow-heel and spices. There was a dish of potatoes and another of cabbage, with a rice custard to follow.

They were discussing what had to be done during the ensuing week when Ruby suddenly glanced at the window.

"Mabel it's quite dark. Gracious, it's nearly nine o'clock and Mary hasn't come with the keys. She said she hadn't much more to do. What can have happened to her?"

"I'll walk over and see." Mabel collected the plates and put them by the sink. "Leave 'em, Miss Travers. I'll wash t' lot when I gets back."

"I'll come with you." Ruby was already getting her cloak, for the evenings were growing chilly. "I do hope nothing's wrong. I ought not to have let her stay on."

"Don't suppose there's owt amiss." Mabel always put on her black straw hat trimmed with daisies, even if she were only going to walk a dozen yards from the cottage. "Dreamin' of her young man, I shouldn't wonder, and never giving a thought to the hour. Or maybe she simply forgot to drop t' keys in to you."

"I'm sure she wouldn't forget; she's so reliable."

As soon as they got to the edge of the field they could see the blaze. It lit up the sky as if the sun had forgotten its role and had come out instead of the moon, outlining the wooden structure with a reddish glow.

"Oh God, it's the workshop." Ruby started to run. "Mary! Mary! Hurry, Mabel, she may still be inside."

When they got closer they found Jeremy Worsley was already there with some of his father's men. They had seen the conflagration from the manor and had rushed over to see what they could do.

"Mary ..." Ruby could hardly get the words out, for her breath was tearing at her throat like knives. "Mary Skegg was working late. She didn't bring ... the ... the keys back as she should have done. Jeremy, she ... she may be in there."

Worsley frowned for it was obvious that no one could enter the building to effect a rescue and hope to survive. It was too late.

"I expect she managed to get out." He kept a tight hold on Ruby's arm in case she took it into her head to dash to destruction. "She wouldn't ... oh Christ!"

Mabel screamed and Ruby swayed against Jeremy, clutching at his coat. A figure had appeared in the gap where one of Ruby's newly-installed windows had been. It was just a dark shape against the shocking brilliance, flames curling round its head, arms and upper torso like orange feathers. They could hear the faint shrieking above the crackling fury of the fire as it rolled on in triumph. Then the window frame was empty again, timbers falling from the roof to seal Mary Skegg's hot tomb.

"I killed her." Ruby was as white as death, near to fainting. "I left her there and I shouldn't have done. If I'd made her stop when we did, she'd still be alive."

"Of course it wasn't your fault. Ruby, stop it; pull yourself together." Worsley shook the rising hysteria out of her. "You didn't set fire to your own barn."

"Nay, master, but someone did." One of the men had ventured round the back, getting a bit closer to the inferno. "This were set; all the signs over yonder."

Ruby closed her eyes. She had no doubt as to who were responsible. Only a few days she had seen Rowney riding down a lane not far away. She had wondered at the time what he was doing there; now she knew.

As so many weeks had elapsed since she'd burnt Waterfields to the ground to prevent Whitcombe from having it, she thought she was safe. After all, it had been her property and she assumed that the merchant, angry though he'd been, had accepted defeat. But she was wrong. Whitcombe had merely waited for the right moment and then destroyed her livelihood and a pretty young girl into the bargain.

Later, when Mabel had given her tea laced with whisky, she said dully:

"I know who did this, but I'll never find proof. I've lost everything, even Mrs. Pittaway's rings. I took them to work this morning, as usual, to be sure they'd be safe. I forgot all about them and the box with the money in it. There's nothing left but the ten pounds in my purse."

Mabel was red-eyed but in control herself, patting her friend's hand.

"What you going to do? Suppose you can't go on after this. Whoever did it, and I'm not asking 'cos it's nowt to do with me, has got you on the floor this time, may God strike him dead."

It was the spur Ruby needed and at last some colour came back into her ashen cheeks.

"I'm not on the floor, Mabel, not for a minute. If Lionel Whitcombe thinks he's beaten me he's very much mistaken. I'll go to market to-morrow and see what I can buy with my money and perhaps get some credit. Everyone knows I'm good for a loan. I'll shew him it's not that easy to get me down."

"Whitcombe." Mabel was awed. "He's real important, Miss Travers. I wouldn't tangle with him no more if I was you."

"But you're not me." Ruby's lips were tight, her jaw assuming a stubborn line. "I don't care how important he is. Lionel Whitcombe owes me a life and I'm going to make him pay in full."

* * *

The earl was on his way to see Lady Eyre yet again. It was the very last thing he wanted to do, but her peremptory demand for his presence had to be heeded for the time being.

When Wallis had told him she'd become Whitcombe's mistress he could hardly believe it. It wasn't that he'd been gulled by her stout assertion that she had slept with no one since her husband died. Although it was the pose she had adopted in polite circles, he knew quite well how many paramours she had had. But in the past they had always been of unblemished birth and discretion. However, since Wallis had wormed the information out of Farrow, whom he had contrived to meet in the local inn, it had to be true. Gin had loosened the woman's tongue and the result was remarkable.

Stratton finally came to the conclusion that Annora was the kind of woman who liked a rough man between her sheets. He didn't care about her sexual proclivities; he just wanted her to leave him alone.

He was feeling spiritually battered as he cantered along the stony path in the direction of Raygreen. He had spent the last few days at Brindle Mill and it had been atn experience he knew he would never forget. Like everyone else, he'd heard rumours of such places and, of course, the marchioness had wanted to get rid of it. Now he could understand why. She hadn't seen the pain, the tears, the exhaustion and the mangled limbs, but she had sensed the evil.

In addition, he had missed Ruby. If only she could have been with him he thought perhaps the shock wouldn't have hit him so hard. Nothing was quite so bad when she was there to put things into perspective.

When he saw Ruby coming towards him he felt his heart leap like a wild animal loosed from a cage. He forgot Annora, the mill, and everything else as he slid from the saddle and stretched out his hand.

"Ruby, my love, it's good to see you again. The last five days have been an eternity."

He held her for a moment, wondering if his kiss was really all it should have been. Sometimes it was very hard to remember the rules of the game.

Ruby felt peace for the first time since the fire. He healed her with his touch and blessed her with his smile.

"I'm glad to see you too. Just like the first time we met. Me trudging away from a burnt building and you riding along like you were just now."

For the first time he saw the pallor of her face and the look in her eyes.

"What is it? What fire are you talking about?"

"My lovely barn. It's all gone; looms, mules, materials, the lot. But there's something worse. Mary Skegg died; she was trapped, you see."

"Come and sit down and tell me everything. How did the fire start?"

He listened, as he'd listened before, his anger rising as she managed to get through the story. When she began to cry he knew she wasn't lamenting the loss of her loom. She was crying for a girl who had met her death in a terrible way.

He comforted her, not attempting to stem her tears. She needed to shed them and where better than in his arms.

"I'd like to kill Whitcombe," he said when the worst of her grief was over. "Give me leave and I'll call him out."

"No, you can't do that. He'd tell everyone about Cuddy."

"Surely your uncle is out of the country?"

"Whitcombe would still tell people about him and I can't let that happen for mother's sake. I gave her my word. You promised you'd never mention the matter to anyone."

"I didn't promise not to wring his neck for ruining your business and killing one of your workers."

"It's all tied up together. Please, Sebastian, keep away from him. One day I'll deal with him myself, when the chance comes. I won't let Mary's death go unpunished. At the moment, I can't prove it was him."

"Very well, I won't go against your wishes. But you're not to take him on yourself. When the time comes, I will do all that is necessary, or I shan't rest in my grave. What are you going to do now?"

"Start again."

Suddenly his anger dissolved into laughter. She was the same Ruby Travers even in dire adversity; nothing about her had changed. She was as mettlesome as ever and the harder fate buffeted her the more resiliant she became. He said softly:

"My little termagant. Whom are you going to bully this time?"

"Whoever's got the cheapest looms. They'll have to be real bargains because I've only got ten pounds to spend."

"You won't get much with that."

"Then I'll try to borrow. If I can't get a loan, I'll beg or even steal. I'm not going to give up."

He was silent for so long that Ruby looked round at him. Every line and plane of his face was dear to her and she wanted to trace each with her finger. But that would be asking for trouble and she had enough of that already.

"What are you thinking about, Sebastian? You look so sad."

"I was wishing some small part of your fearlessness and perserverance could rub off on the poor wretches in my new mill."

She saw his eyes darken and it was her turn to support.

"Was it very dreadful?"

"It was the most ghastly place I've ever seen. It was like being in the middle of Dante's Inferno. The heat, the noise, the suffocating atmosphere couldn't be matched by anything designed by Lucifer. And the children ... oh Ruby ... the children ..."

"Sebastian!"

She gave him a tight hug, trying to stem his agony. She understood what he was talking about, for she had never forgotten her first sight of Molly Caudle. The girl's story was as fresh in her memory as the day she had heard it.

"I'm sorry. I'm a weakling, I suppose."

"No, you're not." She denied it vehemently. "You care and that's nothing to be ashamed about. I know someone who earns her living in a factory. She told me what they were like and I saw her bruises."

"Words aren't enough." He was gripping her hand, re-living his private purgatory. "One has to see it to know the depths to which we civilised beings have sunk. Ruby, I want you to see it."

It was good to feel his hand in hers again and she was thankful that he was able to speak to her of his horror. She knew he would never unburden himself to a stranger or even let his friends know how he felt. It was because he loved her that he could let down his guard and she was grateful for it.

"I will, if you ask me to, but that won't help much, will it?"

"Yes, if you were there all the time."

"All the time?"

"Yes, if you worked there."

"But I'm a weaver, not a spinner, and I'm an independent. I don't want to spin yarn in anyone's factory, not even yours."

"I'm not talking about spinning yarn." He caught her by the shoulders, his urgency running through her like sharp needles. "The idea has only just come to me, but I'm sure it would succeed. If you were to take a post as supervisor of the women and children, you could protect them from the foremen. I can't be there all the time; I need help. You would have my full authority and anyone who argued with you would lose his job at once."

"It's impossible." Ruby was staring at Stratton helplessly. She had always wanted to do something for the Mollies of the world, but Sebastian's proposal was wholly impracticable. "The foremen wouldn't listen to me, you know that."

"I'd make them and, if I know you, you'd make them listen as well."

"But I wouldn't know what to do. I think it's wonderful of you to try to make the lives of your employees better, but you should look for someone who understands the textile trade. I don't know the first thing about it."

"You don't need to; there are plenty of people to deal with the machines. I want you to be responsible for human beings."

"My dear, it's not that I don't sympathise with them, but ..."

"I'd give you a generous salary and a pony and trap to make the journey from the cottage to the mill. And I'll be there quite a lot of the time to make sure you're all right."

"It's no use. I can't."

"Some of them are only seven or eight, perhaps less. They work up to eighteen hours a day on a small piece of rancid bread. They can only relieve themselves when the foremen take into their heads to let them go. Their clothes are so thin and torn that it's easy to see the welts and cuts which the straps make on their bodies. One small boy had heavy pieces of metal screwed to his ears because he'd made some trivial mistake. He kept shaking his head but that made it worse and he couldn't stop crying. Another was immersed in a tank of icy water because he was still sleepy at five o'clock in the morning."

Ruby was back in the place where she had first seen Molly, aghast once more at the sight of the bruises and contusions on the girl's arms and legs. Then she was in the kitchen at Waterfields, trying not to gape at the way Molly was gulping down the hot food put before her.

"You don't play fair," she said finally, and gave a small shiver. "Where is this mill of yours?"

"The nearest village is Wellsand and the factory is called Brindle Mill."

Ruby sat very still. She had asked Vinnie who would look after Molly's kind until God was ready to do so, and God had answered her Himself.

"Well," she said after a minute, "I can't fight you both."

"Both?"

"I'll explain one day."

"Does that mean you'll do it?"

"I'll give it a try."

"Oh, sweetheart, thank you, thank you."

"It may not work out."

"You'll make it do so, I know you."

"Don't expect too much of me. I'm not very good at miracles."

"I think you are."

Their eyes met, and Brindle Mill with its helpless victims faded from their consciousness as he bent his head to kiss her. For several magical moments nothing mattered but their love, strong and unbreakable, like Ruby herself.

"I said you didn't play fair." Her voice trembled slightly as he released her. "That wasn't a comfort kiss."

"It wasn't meant to be. I starve for you as the children hunger for food."

She didn't want to break the spell which had been woven about them, but she had to for both their sakes.

"Now that you've got Brindle Mill, does it mean you'll be staying on?"

"He came back from paradise with a jerk.

"No. I'll be here longer than I expected, but nothing has changed."

The tiny flame of hope in her was extinguished as if struck

by a chill wind. Then, as always, she braced herself, making the most of the extra crumbs. Sebastian wouldn't be going back to London quite so soon, and she would see much more of him in the next few months.

She rescued her hat from the grass where it had fallen, fastening it firmly on her head.

"Well then, Mr. Clare, if nothing's changed, just you watch the way you kiss me in future."

"I will." He said it gravely, but there was a gleam in his eyes which made her pulse race. "I shall be a model of decorum in future. Can we meet in the wood to-morrow to talk about details?"

"At two o'clock, as usual."

"Two would be perfect. Where are you going now?"

"Home. No point in buying looms if I'm not going to weave, is there?"

"I can't escort you, I'm afraid." He looked away, feeling uncomfortable. "I have a ... business appointment."

She said gently:

"You don't have to pretend, Sebastian. I know about Lady Eyre."

"How?" He was curt. "Who told you?"

"Mary, the girl who died. Her sister is in service with her ladyship."

"Damn gossip and damn ... no, I can't damn the dead, can I? What do you make of my visits to her?"

She was as down to earth as ever.

"I know she wants to marry you, but you can't want to marry her or you'd have done so by now."

His annoyance was once again blown away by her engaging candour.

"Dear Ruby, you are a joy to me, and you're absolutely right. I don't even like her and I'm certainly not going to make her my wife. There is a reason, but it's hard to explain."

"You don't have to tell me what it is."

"This won't affect us, will it?"

"Of course not. What we have isn't going to last for long, so we'd better not let anything spoil it, specially someone you don't like very much."

He drew her to him, ignoring her protests.

"I adore you, do you know that?"

"Yes, I do, but remember the rules."

"To blazes with the rules and confusion to comfort. I needed them once, but I've grown up now. This is a kiss you're going to remember until the day you die. Oh, my dearest, dearest love, what is my life going to be like without you?"

* * *

"You can't do it, Ruby, you can't!"

Jeremy Worsley had listened to Stratton's plan and rejected it out of hand.

"I've given my word."

"Then take it back again. Clare must be mad. The men won't listen to you."

Ruby was inclined to agree, but she'd burnt her boats and she never went back on a promise.

"We can't be sure till I try, can we?"

"Of course we can. You've no idea what these overseers and foremen are like. They're hard, unscrupulous men who think only of how much money they can make and they don't care who suffers as long as their pockets are filled."

"That's exactly why I'm going. To make sure others don't suffer."

"Clare is utterly selfish. Damn him! He had no right to ask this of you."

"I could have refused, but I didn't. It was my free choice. Don't go on about it, there's a dear, for nothing you say will make any difference."

"Tell him you've changed your mind. You know how much I care for you. Marry me and let me look after you."

"I can't do that either."

Worsley shut his eyes as if he were trying to blot out something he couldn't bear to see.

"You love Clare, don't you? I know you've been meeting him. Will he marry you?"

Ruby gave him a straight look, warning him off.

"Yes I love him, and no he won't marry me. It doesn't alter things. I'm not going to cheat you."

"I wouldn't care."

"I would and I can only love one man. Dear Jeremy, let it rest. If you do have kind feelings for me, don't let's talk about this any more. I'll explain just once, so you can see how it is.

"I love Sebastian Clare so much that I would die to save him from a second's pain. He is what makes my heart beat and my soul sing. If I could be his for just ten minutes, I'd be content for the rest of my days. But it can't be and I know it. There's nothing left inside me for anyone else, not even you.

"Accept it, as I have to accept that I'm going to lose Sebastian and with him my reason for existing. It will be like that until I draw my last breath and I wouldn't have it otherwise. As I can't be his, I'll have the memory of him instead. Now do you see why I can't marry you?"

Jeremy had felt only his own jealousy until Ruby had begun to talk about Clare. Only then did he understand the true measure of her love. Her words had made him see passion in a form he'd never known before. Desolate though she was, it was like a prayer to Ruby. To him it was a death-knell.

"Yes, I see. I shan't mention the subject again."

"But you won't take your friendship away from me, will you? It means a lot to me."

"It is yours for as long as you want it."

Her smile was no longer sad, but a testimony to valour and he wanted to cry for her. She saw his expression and laughed, for the mood had to be changed quickly.

"And now you've heard me out, you'll get your reward.

Come on home with me; there's gingerbread for tea."

"And toast and honey?"

"I said you were a pig, didn't I? Oh all right, toast and honey too. I rather think you've earned it to-day."

EIGHT

Ruby arrived at Brindle Mill on a crisp October day. Sebastian was there to greet her and together they made an inspection of every part of the building. Although Ruby had been warned what to expect, Sebastian was right. Words weren't sufficient to paint a picture of what she found. The noise was greater than she had imagined; the smell was frightful; the air so impure it was hard to breathe.

But above all it was the children who brought home to her what mill life was really like. It was terrible to see them scurrying back and forth, pale as little ghosts, bones sticking through their flesh, and very much afraid.

There was an atmosphere of unrest which Ruby sensed almost immediately. Men were surly, not meeting her eyes, and she didn't think it was simply resentment at the new-fangled notions of having a woman supervisor. It went deeper than that and a few more machines had been tampered with during the previous two days.

Stratton had already told the foremen and overseers of her appointment and when he called them together to meet her, she could see their hostility plainly written on their faces. They didn't want a bothersome female interfering in their business. Their grunts warned her that should she attempt to stop the children from overworking she would soon get herself into trouble.

She found Molly Caudle being sick in the one lavatory provided for men, women and children. Normally, as Sebastian had said, females and the young were only allowed to relieve themselves at certain times of the day, so that production was not slowed down, but Molly couldn't wait for the appointed hour.

"Aye, I'm with child," she said in answer to Ruby's concern. "It's Bertram's, but I've not said anything to him, nor shall I, leastways not till I have to. We can't be wed, so what's the point of upsetting him now?"

Ruby nodded, exhorting Molly not to carry heavy loads and promising to do something at once about the food supplied to the workers.

Her baptism of fire came on her second day. Sebastian wasn't there and the foremen, wary of their new master, saw no reason to spare the rod once he was out of the way. A chit of a girl, supposedly caring for the women and youngsters, would be no problem. They intended to ignore her and carry on as usual.

Ruby heard the cries of pain from the other end of the main work area. It was the supreme test and she knew it. In other circumstances she might have been afraid, but a child was being tortured and that was all she could think about as she ran the length of the room. There she found Sidney Price, an overseer, was laying into a nine-year-old boy with uncaring ferocity.

Ruby didn't waste time with orders to stop the punishment, or pleas for mercy. In the noise and confusion her demands would be lost. In any event, Price, bending over to drag his victim nearer, was in no mood to listen.

She simply picked up a stick lying on a nearby bench and brought it down with all her force on the overseer's head. Fury and a kind of madness lent her strength and Price keeled over and lay still.

Although the mules whirred on, human voices faded into a threatening silence as men came forward to form a semi-circle round her. Even an intrepid man might have felt inclined to take flight in such circumstances, but Ruby's temper was still aflame and she knew the moment had come when her success or failure in the job would be decided. She said tautly:

"The next one of you that takes a step nearer to me will get the same, and lose his job. Get back, the lot of you. I want you at your machines in one minute, but before you go hear this. I won't have you touch these children again. The first man who lays a finger on one of them will be out on his ear. In future, arrange your schedules so no one works more than twelve hours a day. There will be proper breaks for meals and decent food provided. If I don't find another privy set up by to-morrow I'll crack a few more skulls. What are you, animals? You're a disgrace to the human race. Now be off with you and watch yourselves, for I'm going to be watching you."

Ruby waited, her breath held in. They were either going to obey and accept future instructions, or they would attack her there and then. After a second or two there was a renewed shuffle of feet and she gripped her weapon, raising it up an inch or two.

"Well, what's it going to be?"

The men looked at her and then at one another. Then with another rumble and a ripe oath here and there they turned away. They had thought her simply one of the master's fancy women, brought in to amuse him during his leisure periods. Now they knew better and not one of them wanted to take on the virago with murder in her eyes and a tongue like the sting of a scorpion.

Ruby watched them go with grim satisfaction. There would be other battles, of course; she had no illusions about that. But she'd won the first, and that was the one which really counted.

Mabel came to see Ruby in the meal-break. Ruby had found her friend a job in the mill and was glad to have her there. She wasn't sure yet whom she could trust, but Mabel's loyalty was rock-solid.

When she had expressed her admiration of the morning's victory, Mabel said:

"Seems you haven't got away from Mr. Whitcombe by coming here."

"Oh?" Ruby was on guard at once. "Why do you say that?"

"I've had me ear to the ground. Some of the women have told me his agents are always hanging around outside. They pay the men for information and get others stirred up by telling 'em they're being put upon by Mr. Clare. No one seems to know why, 'cept he's allus one to get rid of his rivals if he can. With this mill gone, he'd have the whole area to himself and his two factories would get all the profit."

It was alarming, but Ruby remained outwardly calm. Supervisors had to keep their fears to themselves.

"Yes, I expect that's all it is, but we'd better make sure. See what else you can discover, will you? Meanwhile, be a dear and go and have another look at Molly Caudle. I think she's being sick again."

* * *

"I don't think you're even trying." Annora glared at Lionel Whitcombe shrivelling him with her rage. "You said you could close the factory down."

"So I can, m'dear, but not overnight."

"Overnight! You promised to do something in July, and don't forget you've had your payment."

He was soothing, for he didn't want her to turn him away. It was quite true that he'd been dragging his heels, but only because he wanted to enjoy her favours for as long as possible.

"I'm making real headway now."

"You'd better be."

"I am, I am, and don't forget he's not long taken over. Not fair to count back to July." His expression changed suddenly and his voice ws harsher. "'Course, it's not made easier by that damned girl, Ruby Travers."

Lady Eyre gave him a sharp look. He didn't often use that tone in her presence.

"Ruby Travers? Who is she?"

"Stratton's appointed her to supervise the women and children and to keep the foremen and such like from whipping the youngsters. She's a harridan, as I've good cause to know, but that's not all he's done it for, if you ask me."

He was sly, taking the opportunity of slipping the beginnings of a wedge between Stratton and Annora.

"What other reason would he have?" Annora knew he was baiting her, but the question was too important for her to profess indifference. The mention of any woman's name linked with the earl's had to be pursued. "And you haven't told me who she is."

"She was housekeeper to a man called Warren Askwith; then she became a weaver. We had cause to cross swords, she and I, but I've been told she's more than an employee of Clare's. One of the men has seen them walking hand in hand in Owl Wood. Reckon he's real sweet on her."

Lady Eyre whitened, denying the possibility at once.

"Rubbish! I don't believe it."

"Others do, and much as I'd like to see her dead and buried, I've got to admit she's a beauty."

"He wouldn't dare do that to me! Make a creature like that his mistress? No, he couldn't."

"Why not? It's what you did to him." Whitcombe grinned. "Never mind, we're after much the same thing. You want Clare to fail; I want to get my own back on the high and mighty Miss Travers and the mill's as good a place to do that as any. Don't suppose you'd be sorry to see the end of her."

"No, I wouldn't." Annora had got a grip on herself by now, the shock of hearing of Sebastian's faithlessness concealed so that Whitcombe shouldn't gloat. She couldn't understand how such a situation could have come to pass without her hearing about it. Even Farrow had failed to pick up a whisper and that wasn't like her maid. "Indeed, I'd be very glad to see the back of her. First, do what I'm paying you to do. Put Clare out of business; then he'll marry me."

"Unless he fancies Miss Ruby more."

She gave a thin smile.

"Men like Sebastian Clare don't marry weavers, my dear Lionel. How little you know of our world. In any case, by the time the factory is closed, you and I will have dealt with Miss Travers. She could never be his wife, but I'm damned if I'm going to share him with a low-born doxy."

"All right, I'll get on with it." His manner changed to one of fawning adoration for, since he'd become Annora's lover, he was more besotted with her than ever. "See, my dear, what I've brought you to-day."

She ran her eye over the sapphire necklace. It would go well with her newest gown and she didn't want Whitcombe to lose interest in her until his mission was accomplished.

"Very pretty." She was always off-hand when she took his gifts. It was like a form of punishment and she'd soon recognized the masochistic streak in Lionel. "And now, I suppose, another instalment is due."

"I'd do anything for you," he said thickly, as she began to undress. "You know that, don't you. I'd kill for you if I had to."

She lay on the bed, contemptuous of his lust.

"You may have to," she returned bleakly. "If there's no other means of getting rid of Ruby Travers, then killing her is the only answer. Well, what are you waiting for? I haven't got all day."

* * *

By November the mill had become a seething cauldron. Although Ruby had been vigilant, protecting her charges, accidents still occurred. She began to realise that most of them happened in her immediate vicinity, but she kept her nerve. It was probably the overseers trying to get their own back. They'd tire of it soon enough when they saw her indifference.

The men were secretive, whispering in corners. Some of them were afraid of what was happening, but they knew it was more than their lives were worth to inform on those who tampered with machines and were responsible for the insurrection.

Then one day a girl was found dead at the foot of some stairs. A hint had reached Mabel that the young woman had been about to have a word with the master. She had had to be silenced as a lesson to others.

"We must do something," said Ruby. "Things can't go on like this."

Stratton was afraid for Ruby. She made light of the incidents which had so nearly involved her in injury or even death, but he had heard about them just the same. He wished he'd never asked her to take on the job, splendidly though she was doing it.

"I know, but we can't trust anyone here. We don't know who are enemies are."

"We know from what Mabel has said that Whitcombe's got a hand in it somewhere."

"But, like the burning of your barn, we can't prove it. If we could do so, I'd put a bullet through him. No, I must get some men, say six or eight, from outside. I'll go to Burnley to-morrow and should be back by Wednesday. I'll arrange for Wallis to meet them at Fire's Cross on Friday about noon and bring them to see me. There may be last minute instructions to be given."

"But what can men from outside do?"

"Ostensibly they'll be some new spinners I've taken on, but their real job will be to listen to what's being said. With luck, it won't take them long to find out who are the ring-leaders in the mill. Those I propose to hire won't be shy of using their fists if they have to when more trouble breaks out. They'll be an extra protection for you, and they'll break up any concerted movements to damage machines. Ruby, are you sure you ought to stay? I know that I pleaded with you to come, but I hadn't foreseen how things would develop. You pretend that everything's all right, but I know what's been going on. You're in constant danger, you know that."

She smiled, brushing his fears aside.

"I can look after myself. The men may be hacking your mules to pieces, but they're not keen on taking me on."

"You've been wonderful." He knew she was playing down the truth for his sake. It was yet another example of her unflagging fortitude and he wanted to kneel at her feet in admiration. "I wish I could kiss you."

"Not during working hours, whatever next? Go about your business, Mr. Clare, and let me tend to mine. And Sebastian."

"Yes?"

"Be careful. If Whitcombe is behind all this it could get very nasty. Do you think he's doing it because I'm here?"

"No, I'm sure he isn't. He doesn't like the idea of Brindle Mill becoming successful. It would mean competition for his own factories. I've been told this isn't the first time he's wiped out the opposition. There was a mill a few miles away from one of his. He paid workers to do just the same thing there, but I'm not going to let him do it to me. He's bitten off more than he can chew this time. He can't appear in the picture himself; he has to bribe some of the more unscrupulous spinners. We'll know who they are when my men get here, and then we can send the guilty ones packing."

"If you're sure. I thought perhaps it was to pay me back for Waterfields."

"I don't think so. Even he wouldn't go to these lengths to persecute you. After all, he's already ruined your business. That should have satisfied him."

"It would be enough for most people, but I'm not sure about Whitcombe."

"Put it out of your mind. This is a straightforward case of intimidation and dirty under-hand moves to get the whole cake for himself. Look after yourself until I get back."

"I will."

"Ruby."

"Yes?"

"I love you."

Whilst Ruby was hushing Stratton, Molly was standing outside the small room which Ruby used as her office. She had been sent with a message for the supervisor but, finding her with Clare, had waited uneasily for the conversation to finish. She couldn't help but hear what was said, for the door was half-open. She felt bad at eavesdropping and was about to turn away when Mabel Birtwhistle said sharply:

"What are you doing here, Molly Caudle?"

Molly jumped, turning red as if she were a felon caught out in an unlawful act.

"Just came to give Miss Travers a message, is all."

"And hanging about listening to things not meant for your ears? Give me the message and then get back to your work."

Mabel, now in charge of the food and sanitation arrangments, together with first-aid for those injured on the factory floor, went back to the newly-formed kitchen and started to spread dripping on thick slices of bread.

She was very uneasy about the air of menace which had pervaded the mill during the last few weeks. It wasn't just the accidents or the spoiling of the machines. It seemed to her that there was something much more serious going on, but all her enquiries had proved fruitless. The women who had once talked to her now shied away, nervous as kittens.

She wasn't too happy about the relationship between Ruby and the master either, not that it was her business as she was always reminding herself. Still, Miss Travers was like a sister to her and she didn't want her to end up with a broken heart. Mr. Clare was as handsome as they came, with the air of of lord, but he wasn't the sort of marry a weaver or even a supervisor.

"Oh, my chick," she said under her breath as she reached for a tin platter. "Don't do nothing foolish. Can't say I knows much about men, but one thing's for sure. Like my old ma used to say, you can't trust the best of 'em a bluddy inch. You just remember that, lass, or next time it'll be more 'un your barn what gets burnt."

* * *

When Seth Monger, an odd-job man working round Annora's house, was asked by her to undertake a small favour for her, he leapt at the chance. The money was generous and he was fond of drink and women, prepared to go to any lengths to earn enough to pay for both.

It wasn't difficult for him to discover where the new supervisor at Brindle Mill lived. He was acquainted with a number of the workers at the factory and a few coppers got him all the information he needed. He had no scruples as far as his task was concerned, but he did wonder what the girl had done. There had been real venom in Lady Eyre when she had given her instructions. He shrugged the reason aside; it was nothing to do with him.

It was late on a November afternoon when he set out to fulfil his promise. Mabel Birtwhistle had gone to visit a friend and Ruby had washed her hair, taking a leisurely bath in front of the kitchen fire. As no one was about, she went up to her bedroom wrapped only in a towel, unpinning her hair and letting it fall about her shoulders. She discarded her makeshift wrap and was reaching for a shift when she heard the slight sound behind her.

She spun round, her heart hammering as she saw Monger's grin. He was tall, with a thatch of red hair and black mischief in his eyes.

"Very nice," he said appreciatively, taking his fill. "Aye, reet nice."

"Wh ... who are you? How dare you come in here?"

"Don't matter much who I am, leastways, it won't when we get down to things."

"Get out!"

"Not me, lass. Just you come here and let's have a bit o' fun."

Ruby cried out, but the next second Seth had his hand

over her mouth and no matter how hard she struggled, she couldn't release herself from the iron grip round her waist. Flat on the bed, she fought as best she could until Monger grew tetchy.

"Enough of that, you bitch. Best take what's coming to you or it'll be the worse for the earl. He could be the next to have an accident. Might mean the end of 'im and you wouldn't want that, would you?"

He removed his hand and Ruby gulped in air. It was a mistake after all. She didn't understand the reference to an accident, but the fierce-looking creature manhandling her thought she was someone else, for she had never met an earl.

"Leave me alone, you hateful wretch. I'm not who you think I am. I don't know any earl. Let me go and get out of my house or I'll …"

"You'll what?" He scoffed, confident of his strong position. "You won't do nothing, my hoity toity Miss. As for the earl, you know 'im right enough. I've 'eard tell 'ow you walks in Owl Wood with 'im."

Ruby lay back stunned, not fighting any more. She felt as if someone had poured icy water all over her, chilling her to the bone. She couldn't accept what the ruffian was saying, yet he seemed so sure of himself. But Sebastian wouldn't have lied to her; it wasn't in him to do so.

"Owl Wood?"

"Ah, you remembers now, do you? Sebastian Clare, Earl of Stratton, and master of t' mill. A grand and high-born buck he is to be sure. Sweet on 'im, are you? Well, what's good enough for his lordship's good enough for me. Come 'ere, you pretty she-devil; let's 'ave a kiss."

Sebastian was returning from Burnley when he came to Ruby's cottage. He saw the lights and decided to break his own rule. Just this once he would call on her and, after all, it was a matter of business which had taken him to the market town.

The front door was open but Ruby wasn't in the kitchen

or the parlour. He called to her, getting no reply. He hesitated before mounting the stairs, but his need to see her was growing by the minute. Just a quarter of an hour with her wasn't much to ask.

When he walked into the bedroom it was as if someone had struck him hard on the back of the neck. He looked at Ruby, naked on the bed, and then at the man hastily pulling up his breeches. He felt the man brush past him, rushing away from trouble, hearing the foul oath spat in his direction.

He stood very still when the front door slammed. The blood was pounding in his temples, his limbs leaden and immobile. He wanted it all to be a bad dream from which he would soon awaken, but it wasn't a nightmare. It was real.

He was stunned by his own blindness. Ruby was the first woman who had broken through the barriers which guarded his heart. He had cast aside his normal reserve as he had poured out his need for her. She had made him vulnerable; she had also made a buffoon of him.

In that dreadful moment as he stared at her with dead eyes, it was as if a series of pictures was flashing through his mind. They passed swiftly, one by one, like shadows on a screen, yet each was crystal clear to him.

He remembered their first meeting, when she had bent over him full of concern: their second encounter, as he had pushed her cart for her and told her that her hat was on crooked. Then came the remembrance of how it had been when he touched her lips with his own, followed by his admission that he loved her as he had loved no woman before.

She had been so many things to him. Sometimes she had seemed like a child; on other occasions endearingly maternal as she comforted him. She could be severely practical or almost ethereal, depending on her mood. Her valour was a bright star and he had been dazzled by its light. She had made him laugh many times; now and then she had brought him near to tears. He had called her his darling girl, and they had shared magical moments which would never come again.

It was hard for him to accept that it had all been a sham. It was well-nigh impossible to believe that his Ruby wasn't what she had appeared at all. She was not a warm and wonderful human being. She was a detestable shell, corrupt and rotten inside, and as clever at theatricals as Sarah Siddons.

He tried to be fair, even as disgust and terrible disappointment washed over him like pitch. She didn't belong to him; he had told her quite plainly that he couldn't marry her. Perhaps it was unreasonable of him to expect her to be faithful, yet she had said that nothing mattered as long as they could be together for a short while. She had also said he was the only one for her, and he had believed her.

He had known from the beginning that they wouldn't have long, his only consolation being the memories she would leave with him. Now she had crushed those under her heel and left him with nothing.

Under the shattering misery was the knowledge that he would never be able to trust a woman again. If Ruby, his immaculate and flawless beauty, was false, then every other female he ever met would be suspect.

Even in his shock and pain the sight of Ruby's body overwhelmed him. It was everything he had expected it to be and he wanted her so badly that it was like a terminal sickness. It was then that his agony turned to rage.

At first he had it under control, raising his quizzing-glass and letting his gaze run slowly over her.

"Forgive me, madam," he said finally. "I fear I am a trifle *de trop*."

Ruby's face had drained of colour and her mind was a complete blank. The suddenness of the attack on her, and the fact that Sebastian hadn't told her the truth, left her bereft of speech. The unknown intruder had made her feel dirty and despoiled. Sebastian's contempt was dragging her down further into the mire. Somehow she managed to reach for the sheet, covering herself as she forced words through parched lips.

"It ... it isn't what you think."

"Oh?" He used sarcasm to shield the wounds which were bleeding where she couldn't see them. "How odd, but perhaps my eyes were deceiving me. I could have sworn that you and your companion were copulating on the bed."

The condemnation in his eyes told her that he had judged her and found her guilty. She had no chance of making him believe the truth, yet somehow she had to try. She wanted memories, too, but not like these.

"I swear we weren't. He came in so quietly I didn't know he was there until he was just behind me. I ... I ... don't even know who he was. I was trying to get away from him when you ..."

"You weren't moving. You were quite still beside him."

They looked at one another, the silence like a shroud. Both realised the extent of their loss and neither knew how to deal with it.

"Not at that moment." Ruby broke the bitterness of the spell. "That was because he had just told me who you were, and I was numb. Why didn't you tell me you were the Earl of Stratton!"

"Why didn't you tell me you were a whore?"

She flushed, trying not to let the stinging lash of his words make her cry.

"You have no right to call me that."

"Why not, it's what you are. You were flaunting yourself for that oaf's benefit, letting him put his hands all over you. You weren't resisting him; you were enjoying it."

Ruby's world was crumbling round her, but she put up another fight.

"I wasn't enjoying it. I hated it; hated it! Nothing like that has ever happened to me before, and it wasn't my fault. Don't blame me for something I had no part in."

He was full of spite, the fury in him rising to storm proportions.

"Oh come, it's clear enough what you were doing. Because I put you on a pedestal and wouldn't take advantage of what I believed was your innocence, you looked elsewhere for satisfaction and let me make do with comfort kisses. Comfort kisses! Christ, what a clown I've been. And I don't suppose that swine was the first either. I've heard how Jeremy Worsley pays court to you. Do you sleep with him, or is he as big a dupe as I am?"

"Jeremy is a friend, nothing more." She knew she had lost him and prayed that he would go before she gave way. "As for that man – I swear I've never seen him before."

Suddenly the dam broke and Stratton took three quick strides to the bed.

"Liar! You damned, hypocritical little liar. You're wasting your time, for I prefer to rely on the evidence of my own eyes."

"It's the truth! I don't know who he is."

She saw the glitter in Stratton's eyes and was terrified of him. Only once before had she seen anger in him, when she had told him about Whitcombe and his threats. That paled to insignificance against his present humour.

"Ah yes, your customer." His smile was a travesty. "I fear I've driven him away, but perhaps I can satisfy your needs instead. My mistresses tell me I'm rather good in bed, and obviously so are you. The next fifteen minutes should be most enjoyable.

Ruby gasped as the sheet was ripped away from her, trying to pull back as the earl caught hold of her. When she looked into his face she shuddered. The man whom she had adored was no longer there. It was a stranger who straightened up and loosened his stock. Her throat was as dry as dust and she could hardly swallow, for she could see how dangerous he was.

"Don't ... please don't ..."

"So coy?" He mocked her as he removed his coat. "There's no need to go on play-acting. I've had enough of that for one day."

"I wasn't play-acting and keep away from me." Her fingers curled round the heavy candle-stick on the table beside her. "Go away, or I shall ..."

He moved like lightning. In another second the candle-stick was clattering against the opposite wall and he had her pinned down. She had had no experience of men, but she knew that what Sebastian was doing to her wasn't love-making. Every stroke and caress was a studied insult, meant to sully her.

"Don't ..." She knew he wasn't listening, but she pleaded anyway. "I loved you; I still do. Please believe me."

"I don't, nor do I want your grubby affection. But I'll take your body as payment for making a fool of me. You chose the wrong one to trick this time, my dear."

He caught her to him again, his kiss like nothing she had known before. Her lips were bruised by his savagery, her breath knocked out of her by his weight on top of her. She knew she was being punished, albeit for something she hadn't done, but she couldn't save herself.

Then, quite suddenly, it was different. Never in her wildest dreams had she expected to feel as she did at that moment. His violence and brutality aroused in her a sensation she hadn't know existed.

She had thought love was what she and Sebastian had shared since their first meeting. A calm and tranquil relationship, hand clasping hand, and a touching of lips which was beautiful, full of longing, and never cruel.

Now she knew how deluded she had been. The real thing was the raging torrent pouring through her whole being, drowning everything which stood in its path. It was Sebastian's rough hand on her breast, fierce and demanding; the awakening touch of his fingers running down her thigh; his ruthless insistence on total surrender.

Her physical awareness was matched by a soaring of the spirit, her mind reeling with the potent force he had unleashed in her.

She found she was holding him as tightly as he was

holding her, her mouth opening beneath his. Her nails were digging into his back as her hips began to move in a queer, erotic rhythm which she couldn't control. If he had become a stranger, she had changed just as much. She was the whore he had taken her to be, for no decent woman would respond so feverishly to the animal lust which was all he was prepared to offer her.

She could feel her body gradually become a part of his, nearing a frenzied climax which made her moan aloud. Her pride, her dignity, her sense of right and wrong had faded away. All that was left was raw and primitive desire.

When the earl raised his head, his grasp slackening, Ruby felt as if she had fallen from a great height. A moment before she had been in heaven, waiting for the final act which would slake the ravening hunger in her. Now the transcendental enchantment had slipped away from her, because he was not going to finish what he had begun. Sebastian's revenge was worse than anything else he could have devised, and she cried out to him not to go.

Stratton looked at her, not knowing how he had drawn back from the brink. She was the most exciting woman he had ever lain with. He was amazed to find in her such an intense and powerful sexuality. Nothing about her normal mien gave warning of the molten fire he had fanned to life. Her eager and wholly unexpected response had filled him with a craving he could scarcely check. It made him feel ill, because it confirmed the truth about her. He had understood her desperate need, so like his own, but a virgin would have gone on fighting.

She was everything he had ever wanted, but she was also the toy of any man prepared to buy her. As he acknowledged it, something inside him flickered and died.

He rose and fastened his shirt, reaching for his coat. She had not only made him look stupid. She had shewn him the true depths of passion which a man and woman could share. He would never forgive her for that, because it was the one and only time he would experience it.

"My lord." Ruby was watching the ramrod line of his back. "Please ..."

"I've changed my mind." He gave her an uninterested glance over his shoulder, brusque and withdrawn, as he re-tied his stock. "I can purchase a dozen like you any time I want them."

He saw moisture on her cheeks and the droop of her lips. They made her look like the young girl with whom he had fallen in love and he almost gave in, but not quite.

"All that I said was true." She knew it was hopeless but she couldn't let him leave her without one more try. "I'm not what you think I am."

He walked to the door, turning to deliver the *coup de grâce*.

"Oh yes you are," he said softly. "I've known many women, but none with such a talent as yours. You're a born strumpet and I'm a credulous blockhead. I said I was rather good at this sort of thing, didn't I? I congratulate you, madam, you are better still."

He went out into the cold evening, wishing his life was over. It had no value to him if Ruby wasn't there to be part of it. She could only have been in his dreams, once he had left Lancashire, but now she had snatched even that tenuous link from him. He wondered why he hadn't raped her, as he had fully intended to do when his temper flared, for she had deserved it. When he knew the answer he closed his eyes, letting the hurt take over again.

It didn't matter what she was, or how she had cheated him. What he felt for her could never be recaptured with any other woman. She had been his beginning; she would also be his end.

Ruby lay quietly for some time after the earl had gone. She was utterly drained and painfully unfulfilled. Later, she knew she would be appalled by the way she had behaved. She would grieve because she would never feel Sebastian's touch again or see the devotion in him. She would mourn the loss of his smile, which was more precious than gold, and the joy of his embrace. If she walked in Owl Wood in the future it would be alone, for Sebastian had gone.

But these emotions and regrets were for another day. Just then, all she could think about was his kiss which had kindled the wildness in her, and the fact that she had so nearly become his.

It had been a devastating way to grow up, but exhilarating too. She would remember every detail of the encounter, even when she was old and love had become a word without a meaning.

At last she sat up. Things had to go on as before. She would walk and talk; work and sleep; eat and drink; laugh and cry, but it would never be the same again. She would be a puppet, going through the motions of living as if someone were pulling strings attached to her arms and legs. Inside, she would be hollow and barren as she cried for the man she could never have.

"Sebastian." She said his name aloud, hoping he would hear it in his heart. "Whatever you think of me, I shall never stop loving you. Oh, my dearest, dearest Sebastian, please tell me how I can survive without you."

NINE

"Fire's Cross, eh? On Friday?"

"That's what master said, sir. About noon."

"How many was Clare going to hire?"

"Six or eight."

Lionel Whitcombe looked at Molly Caudle thoughtfully. She was thin, shabby and very pale, hunching her shoulders as she perched on the stool he had offered her. He wasn't a man who normally noticed the condition of his fellow man. Unless they were of importance to him, like Lady Annora, he wasn't interested. But something about the girl got through his thick skin. He couldn't remember seeing defeat so clearly written on any human being's face before.

Molly didn't look at Whitcombe, but at her hands clenched in her lap. If someone had told her that one day she would betray Miss Travers she would have laid about them with a stick, for she owed Ruby so much. But that was before disaster struck.

Things had been going from bad to worse for some time. At three months she had had a fall. She hadn't lost the baby, but since then she had grown weaker and less able to work. A few days before Molly made her momentous decision to see Whitcombe, Ruby had spoken of laying her off until after the baby came. Molly's heart had sunk, but she didn't blame Miss Travers. Everyone had to earn their wages. For the past two months she and Bertram had both had idle spells because their machines had been put out of order, and their money had dried up. Ruby's loan had long since been spent, and the landlord was threatening again. There was neither food nor heat in the cottage and Timmy, shivering one minute, sweating the next, was slipping away in paroxysms of coughing.

She hadn't been able to hide her condition from Bertram after all. He had heard the other girl's whispering and had confronted her, demanding the truth. He had insisted that they should get married, home or no home. No child of his, he said firmly, was going to be born out of wedlock.

But the wedding-day had never come, for Bertram had been taken to prison two weeks before. Out of his mind with anxiety for Molly and the children, he had stolen food and candles from a shop, together with money the proprietor kept in a tin box behind the counter. He was caught at once, for he wasn't used to crime, and the neighbours were quick to assure Molly that it would mean transportation for him, as he had no influential friends to speak up for him.

She waited until Bertram had been in gaol for fourteen days before taking the final step into spiritual degradation. Beatie had been whimpering all night, doubled up with the pangs of hunger. Fergus didn't cry, but his unwavering gaze on his elder sister told her that she had failed him and the others. He didn't know about the coming infant, but she agreed with his judgment. It had been up to her to do something, but she was no longer able to cope.

The idea of never seeing Bertram again, or at least not for many years, plus a visit on the previous evening from the owner of the cottage, issuing his last warning, had tipped the scales. It was Bertram and the children or Ruby Travers, and Molly knew where her duty lay.

"Say anything else, did he?"

Molly came back to the present, raising her head at last.

"Not much. Like I told you, the men are to pretend to be ordinary spinners. They'll watch to see who's making trouble and Mr. Clare said they wouldn't be slow to use their fists." Molly didn't think it was necessary to add that Mr. Clare and Ruby had talked of Lionel Whitcombe and their suspicions of him. She had gone far enough and was very tired. The room was swimming round her, but she knew she mustn't faint or her treachery would be for nothing. She had walked a long way to get to Mr. Whitcombe and all her hopes were pinned on him. Everyone knew he was paying men at Brindle Mill for information, and other things. She had put her knowledge before him; now she wanted her dues. "You will speak to the magistrate, sir, won't you? You're such an important man that he'd listen to you and let Bertram go."

"Doubt that. Corbin stole, didn't he?"

"Only 'cos me and the children are so hungry. I'm pregnant, you see, and they've said I must go soon; I can't work fast enough now."

"He won't get off without punishment, whatever I do."

She could feel suffocating heat run through her, despite the coldness of the day. It was always the same when she was about to be sick, and she had to hurry or it would be too late.

"But what I told you is worth something. I didn't want to tell on Miss Travers or the master, but I thought you'd help me if I did. Folk say you're a fair payer."

"Aye, but you're asking a lot." He wanted to get rid of the girl, for she had served her purpose. Still, he didn't want hysterics and floods of tears, so he lied. "All right, since you've done me a favour I'll do you one. I'll talk to the magistrate and see if he'll use his influence to get the boy kept in England to serve his sentence. Might persuade him to go easy on him too."

Her fervent gratitude and utter relief caused him a passing qualm, for he had no intention of intervening in Corbin's case. The man was a robber and deserved all he was going to get. If it had been left to him, he'd have had the rogue strung up.

To his everlasting surprise he found he was handing Molly a few coppers. Although he spent a fortune on his women, he couldn't remember giving a pauper anything before. The wench hadn't asked for money, but her need for it was obvious. It made him feel as if he'd kept his end of the bargain. He now knew what Clare was up to; she had sixpence to spend.

For most of the journey home Molly wept. Many times during her exhausting walk she wished she hadn't gone to the merchant. She had hoped her perfidy would result in Bertram's release, but Whitcombe had made plain there was no chance of that. But as long as he wasn't sent to a penal colony, she didn't mind quite so much. If he stayed in the country maybe she could visit him now and then. It wasn't nearly as bad as the other side of the world, and perhaps Whitcombe's influence would shorten the sentence.

Her only other course would have been to ask Ruby for more help, but she'd always hated begging. This way she kept shreds of her tattered pride, for she had sold and Whitcombe had purchased. It wasn't charity.

When she had bought two loaves of bread and some milk in Wellsand village she climbed wearily up the slope towards the cottage. In the half-light it seemed to her that Miss Travers was standing there, not angry but puzzled as she put a question to the girl to whom she had given succour.

"Why, Molly, why?"

"'Cos I had to," said Molly aloud as the apparition vanished in the mists covering the hills. "I never meant you no 'arm, you least of anyone. Oh, Miss Ruby, forgive me, forgive me. There just wasn't nothing else I could do."

* * *

Late on Friday afternoon Sebastian Clare braced himself and went into Ruby's office. He didn't want to see her, but she had to be told what had happened at Fire's Cross. He used the same air of nonchalant indifference which he'd tried on his father the day the latter had sent him out to London.

Ruby had prayed he wouldn't come near her, at least not

for a while. She needed time to grow a shell behind which to hide, but he hadn't given her the chance for that. She could feel herself trembling, making sure he wasn't aware of it.

"My lord." She was very formal. "Can I do anything for you?"

"I think that is highly improbable. I merely came to inform you that my men ran into an ambush to-day at the place where Wallis was waiting for them. Two were killed, three injured. They went straight back to Burnley, taking their dead with them."

"Oh no!" She forgot her own feelings in her dismay at the news. "How dreadful. What about your valet? Was he hurt?"

"A few bruises, but he'll be all right. He saw nothing until some two dozen men came streaming out of the nearby wood. It was carefully planned."

"By Whitcombe, do you think?"

"Almost certainly."

"What will you do now?"

"Go and see him and put an end to this once and for all."

She wanted to tell him to be careful, but she no longer had the right to be solicitous. Even if she could think of the proper things to say, the words wouldn't be welcome. He would simply snub her. Instead, she raised a subject she had been dwelling on since the afternoon in the cottage.

"I haven't had a chance to speak to you alone before this. You were away and ..." His air of boredom wasn't helping, but she had to get it out. "Do you want me to leave the mill?"

In spite of everything, the idea of her going away brought a sharp protest to Sebastian's lips, but there it died. He looked at her as if he'd never seen her before.

"No, provided your lovers' attentions don't affect your work."

"I haven't got any lovers." In a way she was glad he had flicked the raw place in her heart for it made her angry and that was better than the unbearable grief she had been suffering since their last encounter. "You have no right to …"

She stared at the door, her protest hanging in mid-air. Sebastian had walked away from her, not even bothering to listen to the end of the sentence.

"Just seen Mr. Clare," said Mabel, coming in with a cup of tea. "Looked right angry, he did. Don't hear much about what's going on these days, but I were washing up t' pots when two of the men started talking outside in the passage. They didn't know I was there, of course, or they'd have shut up. Seems there was a fight of some sort at Fire's Cross to-day. Word is that master were bringing in some men, but they were expected. Sounds as if it were a proper rumpus from what them spinners were saying."

"Two dead, three injured; the rest went home." Ruby pushed her torment away, explaining to Mabel what Stratton had planned. "The thing is," she finished, her brows coming slowly together. "How did anyone find out? When Mr. Clare told me what he was going to do, there was no one else in this room."

Mabel was thoughtful.

"Maybe there weren't no one in the room, but there was someone outside it. I saw that Molly Caudle listening at the door; it weren't shut, you see. I noticed her from other end of t' workshop. I reckon she'd been there some time. When I asked her what she thought she were doing, she turned as red as a beetroot and said she'd got a message for you. I soon sent her packing."

"But Molly would never do such a thing, especially as I was involved, in a way. She's fond of me, I'm sure of it."

"Likely she is, but that girl's at the end of her tether. She's having a bad time carrying her baby, and the fall didn't help. She's had to be laid off with others when machines weren't working, so money's tight. Then, to cap it all, that boy of hers, Bertram Corbin, stole for her and he's in prison. What with that, and her brother near to dying and a sister sick, I guess she'd do anything for a bit of money to buy food and pay the rent. Daisy Froome told me only t' other day that landlord's threatening to turn 'em out of the cottage. Seems Molly thought you intended to get of her permanent like. Placed like that, I guess any woman would act against her better nature to try to remedy things."

"Why didn't she come to me?" Ruby's sense of failure swamped other thoughts for the time being. "I had no idea what had happened to Bertram, but it's true I said I thought she ought to stop working until the child came. I should have realised what that meant financially. It's my fault, Mabel. I was so busy thinking of my own affairs I didn't bother to ask if Molly was managing."

"She's not your responsibility."

"Yes she is. Where is she now?"

"Not come in for last two days."

"I'll have to try and get to see her, soon as I've got a moment."

"What'll Mr. Clare do now?"

Mabel watched in consternation as Ruby's eyes filled with tears. She'd seen the unhappiness in her friend in the last day or two, but she'd kept her questions to herself. If Miss Travers wanted to tell her anything, she would. Meanwhile, it was best to keep a still tongue in one's head.

"Not Mr. Clare. He's the Earl of Stratton. He didn't feel able to tell me that himself and now ... well ... he's going to see Whitcombe. Oh God, I wish I could ..."

"Can I 'elp you, luv?"

Ruby looked at the affection and concern in Mabel's tired eyes and shook her head.

"No, I'm afraid you can't; no one can. It was so beautiful while it lasted, but now it's over. Oh, Mabel, have you ever wished you were dead?"

Sebastian was sitting by the fire when Wallis came in with Lady Eyre's message. He was greatly concerned by what had happened at Fire's Cross, planning to go to Burnley the next day to see about compensation. But his sense of lifelessness had another cause. That was due to losing Ruby.

Wallis could see that his master was a thousand miles away, withdrawing very quietly and without a word. Whatever was gnawing at the earl, the latter wasn't able to talk about it yet.

Stratton stared into the flames where Ruby's face looked back at him. He hoped he would soon forget what she looked like, but he knew he never would. He told himself it wasn't really a loss at all, for the girl he had worshipped had never existed. She had been no more than an illusion but, for all that, she had filched his heart and left him for dead.

To take his mind off his afflictions he opened the letter. It was another invitation to dine and his mouth twisted. If he failed in business, as now seemed very likely, at least one person would be pleased. He'd promised Annora that should such a state of affairs come to pass, he would talk to her again about marriage. She would expect him to do so, although he'd no intention of bestowing upon her the illustrious name of Clare.

When the truth dawned on him it was like a cloudburst, all the pieces rushing together with neat precision. It caught him wholly unawares and made him swear aloud. He should have seen it from the start, because it was really so obvious. He had been blinded by love and his normally acute perception had suffered as a consequence.

What had been happening was nothing to do with Whitcombe's greed in commerce. It was about Annora and her desire to become the Countess of Stratton.

He remembered his incredulity when he'd learned that Annora had become Whitcombe's mistress, assuming she fancied a plebian master in her bed instead of her usual tame mice. She'd always told him most emphatically that she'd led the life of a nun since her husband died. It was a ludicrous claim, but she'd made it to hide from him the fact that she was a high-class badger. Then, unbelievably, she'd thrown away all caution and given herself to Whitcombe almost under his, Stratton's, nose.

But she hadn't gone to bed with the merchant for a romp.

She'd paid him with her body to close down Brindle Mill and thus force the marriage question into the open again. She was unscrupulous and fanatical enough to use such a method, and he had to admit that under her shoddy exterior she had genuine love for him.

As for Ruby. He winced, even at the thought of her name. Whitcombe hated her enough to maim or kill her if he got the chance. She hadn't thought one burnt barn had settled the score and she was probably right. He realised then, without a doubt, that Annora knew about Ruby and his relationship with her. Annora was notoriously jealous and the elimination of a rival would have become part of her contract with her new lover.

He got up slowly, throwing the note into the fire. he had intended to go and see Whitcombe that afternoon; now his plans had changed. Lionel Whitcombe could wait; Lady Annora Eyre could not.

* * *

Annora was in a restless mood. It was taking a long time to bring Sebastian to heel and she was profoundly bored with Lancashire and the discomforts of her friend's house. Seth Monger claimed to have done her bidding, but he had looked shifty. She told herself there was no need to fuss. Monger was by nature a sly man and there was no reason why he shouldn't have carried out his orders.

It was good to hear from Lionel of the rout at Fire's Cross. He had passed on to her the information given to him by Molly Caudle and she had to admit that Whitcombe had moved with speed and efficiency to block the earl's counter-measures.

But it was all so slow and she wanted Sebastian then, not in six months' time. She had always known he wasn't in love with her, but even that slight to her pride didn't alter her feelings for him. She wanted him to much it was painful just to look at him. She knew she was a fool, but there was nothing she could do about it.

When the earl was announced her ennui vanished.

"Sebastian, how glad I am to see you. I was feeling particularly low a moment ago. It's these Northern parts, of course. So uncivilised. Now you're here I'll feel better."

"I doubt that."

"Oh?" Her smile faded as she looked at him. He never gave her the warm smiles she longed for, but on the other hand he'd never looked as sternly at her as he was doing now. It sent a shaft of doubt through her, but she was too much in control of herself to let him see it. "Why is that, my dear?"

"Because I'm about to tell you exactly what I believe you and Lionel Whitcombe have been doing at Brindle Mill and why you, in particular, are engaged in such activities."

"I've no idea what you mean." Her protest was a perfect mixture of surprise and innocence. "Really, you are behaving in the most extraordinary manner. So farouche and unpleasant. As for this man Whitcombe ..."

"Shut up!" He was curt, abandoning all ceremony. "For once hold your tongue and let your ears alone do you service."

She listened in silence, wondering how best to handle him. His voice was colder than it had ever been before, the extent of his knowledge was remarkable. When he mentioned Ruby Travers there was only a flicker of difference in his expression, but it was enough. Annora spotted the change and it was all she could do to stop herself from screaming at him. She forced herself to remain calm and to continue ignorance of his accusations.

"You're being ridiculous. It's all in your imagination."

"Do you want me to walk out of this house and never see you again?"

"No!" The exclamation was wrung out of her because she could see his threat was a real one. Whatever she had to say or do to keep him, she would face it as best she could. What she couldn't contemplate was losing him altogether. "No, don't do that."

"Then admit that what I've said is true. You and Whitcombe are trying to put me out of business so that I shall come back to you, begging for the sanctuary of your bed and the comfort of your money-chests. Be warned, Annora. If you lie, you've seen the last of me."

She knew there was nothing for it and for once set aside pretence and guile.

"Very well, it's true. I only did it because I love you so much. It seemed there was no other way to bring you to your senses."

The lines round the corners of Sebastian's mouth made her shiver.

"Then let me make something plain to you. I won't consider marrying you until Brindle Mill flourishes and all the problems are gone."

"That isn't what you said before. You told me ..."

"I know what I said, but circumstances have altered. The sooner you put an end to all this the sooner your wedding day will dawn. And leave Ruby Travers alone."

Triumph at the mention of her wedding day warred with her hatred of the girl she had never seen, but who had become her bitterest enemy. Jealousy won, for the sound of Ruby's name on the earl's lips was like a cut of a whip across Annora's heart.

"You and that cheap little trollop! Did you think I wouldn't hear about her and how you go walking in the woods with her? How can you be so stupid? She's trash. Why else would she tumble in the blankets with a clod like Seth Monger?"

The earl's eyes dilated as the shock waves hit him, almost rocking him back on his heels. He could hear again the insults he had hurled at Ruby, remembering the ugly things he had done to her body until, in spite of his vindictiveness, their mutual desire had lifted them to a state of pure ecstasy. When she had cried out to him to believe her, he had turned his back and walked out.

"Sebastian? Why are you looking like that?"

The room came back with a rush and he said very softly:

"How did you know Monger had been with her?"

Annora's colour faded. In her fury she had betrayed herself, exposing her hatred to Sebastian. She had never intended him to know what she had arranged; it was simply to have been a punishment for the Travers girl. She could feel her heart beating unevenly, for the earl was looking at her as if he would like to strangle her. She tried to make the best of it, pretending someone had told her of Ruby's fall from grace, but it didn't work.

"You could only known about him if you'd sent him to the cottage yourself."

It was no use trying another denial and suddenly she was sick of evasion. If he wanted the truth he could have it, even if it changed his mind about marriage.

"All right, all right, I sent him. I thought she deserved a lesson for her presumption, and I detest the very thought of you touching her. You want honesty; you can have it. I would give you the earth if you asked me for it. There is nothing I wouldn't do to please you, yet you prefer to lie with that bitch."

The earl's anger hadn't abated but he recognised he was seeing Annora as she really was with all the layers of sophistication and affectations peeled away. He was almost sorry for her for loving him; he knew what it was like to love.

"I haven't lain with Miss Travers," he said finally. "Neither did Monger. I didn't know the man's name until you gave it away, but I arrived in time to stop him."

Annora took a deep breath. Her instinct about Seth had been right, but there were more important things at stake just then.

"I've never felt about anyone as I do about you, Sebastian. I'm sure once we are married you'd learn to care for me in the same way. You'll forget all about that girl, because our lives will be rich and full. You're just infatuated with her and that will pass."

"I won't forget her." Sebastian was very calm now, knowing what he had to do and not shirking it. Whitcombe and Annora could still injure Ruby if they put their minds to it and he'd done enough harm already. "I'll love her until the day I die, but I'll marry you, Annora, provided the factory is left alone and you give me your promise not to go near Miss Travers again. Well, what do you say?"

It was the moment she had waited for for so long but the joy was tarnished by his words. If he wanted a promise about his precious mill she would give it to him, but Ruby Travers was a different matter. All the while the girl held Sebastian's heart in her unworthy hands, she, Annora, would know no peace. This time there had to be an accident which was both successful and fatal.

"I agree, darling, of course." She was completely poised again, the ragged ends of her real emotions tucked away once more. "You have my solemn oath that your factory will be all right."

"And Miss Travers?"

Her smile didn't falter.

"Now that you're going to be mine, I've no further interest in her. For me she no longer exists."

Stratton thought she probably meant what she said. The whole lethal exercise had been contrived for one purpose only, but now Annora had got her own way the danger to Ruby was over. He and Annora would marry in due course, return to London, and enter a world in which Ruby had no part to play. But at least she would be safe from the woman who had proved she would stop at nothing to gain her ends.

"So be it, madam," he said, his eyes as chilly as his heart. "We have a bargain, you and I. Now call off your dogs."

* * *

It took Lady Eyre some time to get Whitcombe's agreement to abandon his plan to wreck Brindle Mill. His chief interest was still the undoing of Ruby Travers, for the memory of Waterfields haunted him more strongly than ever. He could feel it mocking him, even though it no longer existed, because it had won the battle. He loathed Travers for snatching away from him what he had hungered for, and he wanted her dead.

"She made a fool of me," he said as he lay beside Annora. "I shan't stop until I've settled my account with her in full. I'll never be right with myself till it's done."

Annora checked her irritation, for that wasn't the way to deal with Lionel.

"I want the same thing, and my account with her is higher than yours. If I can find another way of getting rid of her, will you leave the factory alone?"

"I don't know."

"You'd better know or you'll never come near me again."

That pulled him up short. Annora wore a loose wrap, meant to reveal her ripe beauty, not conceal it. The prospect of not holding her body against his, feeling its pliant and intoxicating warmth, was unendurable. He wasn't worried about Brindle Mill. He could always get hold of that some time in the future when the earl had returned to his life of pleasure in the capital. And if Annora dealt with Ruby Travers there really wasn't much to fight about.

"All right, I'll see the men make no more trouble but you be sure about that whore."

"I'll be sure." Her words were like acid burning holes in the air. "I want her out of Sebastian's life for good and what I want, I get. You've nothing to worry about."

"Suppose not. You wanted Stratton and now you've got him, haven't you?" He wasn't quite won over, for the thought of her marriage ruffled him. "What about me after you've wed him?"

Annora knew exactly what she was going to do about Whitcombe, but she kept her intentions to herself.

"You'll come to London as before, won't you?"

"Aye, but ..."

The wrap slipped from her shoulders and he was as

moved as he'd been on the first day he had seen her nakedness.

"Well then, stop moping. We'll have to be more careful, of course, but these things can always be arranged."

"You mean it." His hands began to wander greedily over her breasts, heat welling up in him as it always did when he touched her. "You promise?"

She longed to thrust the clumsy brute away but she still needed him.

"Everyone wants promises, it seems. Yes, I agree as long as you'll do as I ask. Don't bribe anyone else to smash those stupid machines and leave Travers to me. If you don't I'll get dressed again."

"No! Anything you want, anything. Come here, you hussy, before I burst. Jesus God, you're beautiful!"

* * *

It was while Ruby was sitting with Molly that the message came from the gaol.

Ruby had packed up some provisions and taken them to the cottage on the hillside. Timmy had died the day before and Gwen was losing her hold on life as well. The place was reeking with damp and filled with November fog. When she had handed round the food she sat by Molly scanty bed of sacking, appalled by the look of the girl who clearly was very ill.

She listened with compassion to Molly's tale, not blaming her for going to Whitcombe. If she, Ruby, had done her duty and shewn some Christian concern, there would have been no need for Molly to have sold information to buy bread and seek help for Bertram.

It was Henry Bradley who brought the news, shifting his weight from one foot to the other as he explained what had happened. There had been a fight and by the time the guards had stopped it, Bertram was dead.

"I think I'd like to be alone for a while, Miss Ruby," said

Molly when Bradley had gone, muttering his regrets. "Don't want to drive you off, seeing you've been good enough to come all this way and brought so much stuff for us."

"I quite understand; you don't have to apologise." Ruby bent and gave Molly a light kiss on the cheek. "I know what it's like to lose someone you love."

For a second Molly focused on Ruby's face, the cloud which had engulfed her lifting briefly to shew that the outside world was still there.

"You do?"

"Oh yes." Ruby hugged her cloak tighter about her, sharing Molly's bereavement. Sebastian might not have died in a prison brawl, but she had lost him as surely as Molly had lost Bertram. "I, too, my dear. I'll come again very soon and I'm leaving some money on the table. When you run short of provisions, get Fergus to go to the village for more."

When Ruby had gone, Molly rose and put on her own thin wrap.

"I'm going out for a while, Fergie," she said. "Look after Gwen and Beatie for me, won't you?"

Fergus was still gulping down hunks of bread and jam, but he nodded and she went out into the cold morning, vanishing from sight in the heavy mists.

She knew just where she had to go. It was quite a step to the woods where she and Bertram had first made love, but that didn't matter. Time wasn't important any more. She thought briefly about the children and of Miss Travers, who had been so kind in spite of what she'd done to her. Then everyone else slipped out of her mind but Bertram. He was very close to her, just as he'd been on the first day he'd spoken to her, offering her real bread and butter and laughing at her surprise. Every hour spent with him had been a small miracle and she knew she'd been lucky to have loved and been loved in return.

When she entered the wood she remembered his compassion when she'd told him about Ham Walkden. He hadn't drawn away in disgust; he'd held her close and spoken tender words to her.

She came to a clearing, the fog blowing away sufficiently for her to see the tree which had one of its lower branches dipping down like a beckoning finger. It reminded her of Ham's thick foreginger and the way he had gestured to her to follow him to the store-room.

She looked around until she saw what she wanted. The piece of log was some four foot long and it took her quite a while to drag and heave it into an upright position under the tree. Then she discarded her cloak and began to unwind the rope from around her waist. She had seen it lying in a neighbour's yard only yesterday, and on her way to the wood she had stolen it, as Bertram had stolen money and food for her.

She laid a hand on her swollen belly, her voice as soft as the lullaby she would never sing.

"Don't worry, love," she said and smiled, as if her baby was already in her arms. "I'm taking you with me. I'd never leave you in this rotten world alone. It's not a nice place and the only happiness I ever had in it was with your pa. He's gone, you see, and there'll never be another for me. That's why we're goin', so's we can be with him."

When everything was ready she paused, wondering if she ought to say a prayer. As she was about to commit a mortal sin it seemed hypocritical and she dismissed the idea. God wouldn't help her. Now Bertram wasn't there she'd have to help herself, like she'd done in the old days before he came to look after her.

"Here we go, pet," she said and climbed on to the log, the mist whirling about and filling the clearing again with its malignant presence. "It won't hurt you, I promise. I'd never do nothing to hurt you. You belong to my Bertram and I love you like I loved him."

She paused just long enough to give one more word of comfort to the child she would never see. Then she stepped off the log into space and out of an existence she could no longer bear.

The life and times of Molly Caudle were over.

*   *   *

Jeremy Worsley was out riding when he saw Ruby making her way up the hill. Visibility was poor, but he would have known her anywhere. Although Ruby had made her feelings for him quite plain, he hadn't been able to smother entirely the small grain of hope left in him. When Sebastian Clare was no longer there to bemuse her, something might grow between Ruby and himself which could be cosseted and cared for until it flowered into the next best thing to love.

He thought she had been very subdued for the past few days, but she had proferred no explanation and he had kept his questions to himself. He wouldn't intrude where he wasn't wanted. It had been difficult not to try to help her, for obviously she was sad and low, but patience was his only weapon and he knew he had to wait until she turned to him voluntarily.

As the fog blew back and forth he saw Ruby going into one of the cottages, waiting until she emerged and then following her from some distance. When he saw a man running towards her, his heart missed a beat.

He knew at once that the man was up to no good and dug his spurs in, giving the horse its head. But further down the slope the fog still lay in thicker patches and for a while he lost sight of Ruby and the newcomer. Then he heard her cry out and shouted to her not to worry. His voice was carried away like an echo and he slid from the saddle, hoping to find her more quickly on foot.

When Lady Eyre had sent for Jim Scrope, her under-coachman, she had had no difficulty in getting his agreement to carry out a commission for her. Scrope was young, burly, and not burdened with a conscience. He'd wanted to taste the delights of his employer from the day he'd entered her service and he knew she was aware of it.

The gold coins she had been running through her fingers were welcome enough, but the blatant invitation in her eyes was even more tempting.

The prospect of doing away with Ruby Travers, a girl he'd seen several times near Brindle Mill, didn't bother him at all. He'd killed before and felt no repentance. His first victim had had his neck broken when he took Jim on in a fight; the second drowned in the river as Scrope's thick fingers held him down and let the water fill his lungs. He'd escaped justice because no one else had been present on either occasion. The first death had been laid at the door of the gypsies, the second was considered an accident.

His third essay into homicide had to look like an accident too. Lady Annora had been very firm about that. He had nodded, pocketing his ill-gotten gains and casting a predatory eye over his mistress's voluptuous charms.

He waited for Ruby to leave the mill, pacing behind her. He lay low when she entered one of the cottage, biding his time until she started on her homeward journey. The weather was in his favour and there was a deep clough not half a mile away. Easy enough for someone to lose their way and then their footing.

When he grabbed her, Ruby yelled loudly. She could see in his eyes what he meant to do. She had always known she was in danger, for Whitcombe was an unforgiving enemy. She kicked at Scrope's shins so hard that for a fraction of a second he slackened his grip. It was enough for her and she was away, winging down across rough grass, half-blind, and frightened out of her wits.

When she saw the old hut she made straight for it. She had noticed it on the way up. It looked decrepit and deserted, but it was better than nothing as a refuge. She could hear the heavy footsteps as the man gained on her, her lungs bursting as she tried to quicken her pace.

When she stumbled, she thought she was lost but then Jeremy called out to her and it was the most welcome sound she had ever heard.

"Run, Ruby, run! I'll see to him. Run!"

She needed no second bidding, but as she reached the door of the hut she heard Jeremy cry again. Only this time it was different. It was a shriek of agony and Ruby was numb, not knowing whether to go back to help Worsley or obey his command and get away.

In the end instinct told her to hide. She would have no chance against the man, and Jeremy could be dead already. She fled into the flimsy wooden building, finding it half-full of wood. Like one possessed she shifted some of the logs and stacked them against the door, jamming a stout stake under the latch. She didn't think it would hold for long. Her pursuer was powerful and he had already committed himself to the deed he'd been sent to do. To back away now, leaving her alive to talk, would mean his own end.

She crouched in one corner, a stick in her hand. It wouldn't be much use as a weapon, for as she had pulled away from the man she'd caught sight of something winking in the gloom. He'd got a knife and that was why Jeremy had given that dreadful scream. Next it would be her turn when the door was pushed open with a few kicks and a thrust of massive shoulders.

Suddenly she stood up, putting her hat straight and tidying her hair. If she was going to die, she would do so with the dignity of a human being. She wouldn't go to her Maker huddled in a corner like a trapped rat.

When the banging began she kept her chin up. It wouldn't be long before it was all over. She was sad that she hadn't been able to put things right with Sebastian, but even if there had been time, he wouldn't have wanted to listen to her.

She watched the door open bit by bit. It quivered and creaked at the pounding it was getting, but she didn't move.

Scrope finally pushed the last log out of his way and said gratingly:

"Come 'ere, you bloody sow. Yer friend's dead, so don't look to 'im for 'elp. Now let's see what we can do about you."

TEN

When Sebastian got to the mill to keep the appointment he had made with Ruby he was alarmed to find she wasn't in the building. It had taken him a week to pluck up enough courage to face her at all and he had had countless imaginary conversations with her, all of which had ended in disaster.

If it had simply been a matter of an abject apology he would have grovelled at her feet, begging her pardon for all that he had said and done, but there was more to it than that. In the next breath he would have to tell her that he was going to marry another woman. They had both known it would come to that one day, but had thought of it as something which would happen in the future and in a different place, long after they had parted. To make the announcement now would be like striking her across the face and he wasn't sure he could bear to see the grief flood into her eyes.

There would probably be censure as well as sorrow when she heard it was Annora who was to be his wife. Ruby knew he didn't love Lady Eyre and would assume his decision was made because he wanted riches and an easy life.

"Are you sure she got my note?" he asked Mabel. "Miss Travers is never late."

Mabel was uneasy too. Ruby had assured her that she would be back in plenty of time to see the earl. She might not have thought very much about her friend's delayed returned, had not Rose Whittle and Megan Jones asked who

Miss Travers' new beau was.

"Beau? What beau? What did they mean?"

Mabel was reluctant to tell tales but she hadn't liked the sound of the girls' story and she thought it was just as well the master should know about it.

"Well, they were coming back from Wellsand where they'd been on an errand. They saw Miss Travers walking towards Molly Caudle's house. She were going to visit her. It's not far off and ..."

"Yes, yes." Stratton was impatient for his apprehension was growing. From the moment he had discovered that Ruby wasn't waiting for him he had sensed something was wrong. He didn't know why, except perhaps because she was almost a part of him. Their stormy encounter hadn't made any difference to that; neither had his betrothal to Annora Eyre. "But what about the man ... this beau?"

"They said he were following her, keeping back a bit."

"Why were they so sure he was following her? Couldn't he just have been travelling in the same direction?"

"That's just what I asked 'em, for they're a silly, giggly pair, always minding other people's business. They said that when Miss Ruby stopped for a minute, the man stopped too. They swore he were after her and they'd seen him hanging about outside t' mill in the last couple of days. Seems he'd asked one of the men about her."

Sebastian felt the screw inside him tighten yet again.

"But the fog? Could they really see properly? Are they sure it was the same man who had been enquiring about her?"

"Megan said it were only patchy just there and they described him plain enough. Tall, plenty of muscle, and quite young. I've been trying not to make too much of it, but as she ain't come back as expected ..." Mabel shuddered. "And he had been asking about her. Don't see why he'd do that unless he meant her some harm. Oh, sir, I ought to have done something about this before, oughtn't I?"

Stratton needed no further convincing. His sense of foreboding was too strong to ignore any longer. Annora had promised to leave Ruby alone but Whitcombe hadn't. It was now just a matter of whether he could get to Ruby in time, or whether the merchant's hireling had already done his work.

When Mabel had told him exactly where to find Molly's cottage, he ran the length of the workshop, out of the door, taking a flying leap into the saddle. He knew Ruby couldn't hear him, but he cried out to her just the same.

"Hold on, my love, hold on, I'm coming," he shouted. "Oh dear God, don't let me be too late. Please don't let me be too late."

* * *

Jeremy Worsley regained consciousness almost at once. He was wondering why he was lying on the ground, staring at the grey sky, when the burst of pain hit him.

He tried to get up but it was impossible, and he groaned as memory came rushing back. The man who had stabbed him through the stomach had been after Ruby. He'd probably got her by now and might even have killed her.

One hand moved slowly to his coat pocket, encountering a warm, sticky substance on its journey. At last Worsley felt the comfort of the butt of his pistol, already charged for use. It wasn't wise to travel alone and unarmed and he thanked God he had remembered to pick up the gun before leaving the house. It seemed to him to take forever to pull the cock back until the sear slipped into its second notch ready for firing, but at last it was done.

The world was coming and going in waves. One moment it was there with all its sights and sounds and smells; the next he was in a kind of limbo where there was nothing but cold blackness and acute agony.

Suddenly he heard the man's voice and realised it was very close by. He took a deep breath, praying to the Almighty to give him one more minute of life, for Ruby wasn't dead after all. He could hear her, too, giving her captor a piece of her mind and, although in extremis, he managed a crooked smile. Even in such circumstances as these, Ruby wasn't going to give in tamely.

Scrope's temper was rising, for he hadn't bargained for a shrew like this one. If it hadn't been for Lady Annora's insistence that the girl's death should appear in all respects to be an accident, he'd have cut her throat without further ado. As it was, he would have to get her to the edge of the crevasse before he could be rid of her.

"Shut your mouth, you bawd," he shouted and gave Ruby a shove which sent her sprawling. "I'll give you summat to keep you quiet."

For Jeremy it was then or never, and somehow he managed to roll over on his side. The world became quite still and more in focus than he had ever seen it before. In that second he took in the sweep of the hills, the shapes of the cottages in the background, and Ruby lying on the ground. The man stood out in sharp relief, almost as though the Fates had made a target of him. Every detail of his face and body was easy to read. Heavy shoulders, a thick waist, untidy hair and strong white teeth bared in anger.

He was raising the stick he carried, as if to bring it down on Ruby's shoulders, when Jeremy fired. A look of utter stupefaction spread over Scrope's face as he swayed on his feet. As he pitched forward and lay still, Worsley slumped back, his eyes closing, the flintlock slipping from his fingers.

"Jeremy!"

Ruby picked herself up and rushed to Worsley's side. It was obvious that he was dying and she was filled with a terrible remorse because she had taken his friendship, his love, and now his life, and had given so little in return.

His eyes flickered open when he heard her voice, but he couldn't see her. The darkness was winning the fight, but Ruby was safe and he was content to go then.

Ruby was holding Jeremy's hand and weeping over him

when the earl dismounted and strode over to her. He was filled with a breathless relief to find that she was alive and unharmed. He wanted to take her in his arms and tell her that if she had died, he would have done so too. But the moment wasn't appropriate, for Ruby was saying good-bye to a friend, and his own apologies hadn't yet been made.

"We'll take him home," said Stratton quietly. "He belongs there."

Ruby looked up, wishing she could lay her head against Sebastian's breast and cry her guilt away. He would understand what it meant to have regrets for things left undone. She wondered why he was there and how he had known she was in trouble, but it wasn't the time for questions either.

"He saved my life," she said as he helped her up. "That man over there followed me. He was going to kill me, but Jeremy stopped him."

Stratton went over to where Jim Scrope lay, turning the body over with his foot. He was sorry that he hadn't been the one to pull the trigger, for he recognised the man. He'd him once or twice when he had been visiting Anora, and the extent of the latter's treachery put seeds of murder into his own heart.

"Come." Sebastian's rage was hidden by the time he got back to Ruby. She had enough to contend with at present, and she wouldn't be interested in his abysmal folly. "We must go and tell Jeremy's father what happened. After that I'll take you to the cottage."

"And the other one ... over there?"

"I'll inform the authorities, but as far as I'm concerned he can rot where he lies."

Their eyes met briefly, both tortured by the unhappy meeting, each wanting to hold the other and put the world to rights again.

Then the earl lifted Worsley and laid him across the saddle, turning the horse's head as they began their journey down the hill and in the direction of Coombridge Manor.

* * *

Once Sebastian had become owner of the troubled mill, it was clear to the Marquis of Harworth that one agent wouldn't be enough to furnish him with the necessary information about the difficulties his son was encountering. He gave Edington carte blanche and soon five more pairs of ears and eyes were at work. Report after report streamed into Harworth's study and each was scrutinized down to the last full-stop. When Lionel Whitcombe's name began to appear so regularly, the marquis did a little delving of his own. In London, as in Liverpool, Whitcombe was known and his reputation wasn't enviable in either place.

On a number of occasions the marquis had wanted to ride North with all speed, but he had held back. Stratton had to learn to stand on his own feet and prove what sort of man he was. Although he had been totally opposed to his son dabbling in trade, he had to admit, if only to himself, that the boy seemed to be doing extremely well in spite of everything. With the aid of Miss Ruby Travers, about whom Harworth had made enquiries with quite startling results, Sebastian was holding his own. But the number of accidents was worrying and when men were killed and wounded at Fire's Cross, Clare had had to exercise all his restraint, to avoid interfering.

However, when word reached him that Lady Annora's maid was boasting in the local hostelry that her mistress was going to marry the Earl of Stratton, Harworth had had enough.

"On the assumption that Sebastian hasn't gone out of his mind, why should he offer for Annora Eyre? If our reports shew Whitcombe is her lover, Stratton must surely be aware of it as well."

Oscar had given the matter careful consideration, for it was rather interesting.

"It's known she has a great fancy for his lordship."

"But he no longer has a fancy for her; that's the point.

He's in love with Ruby Travers. His grandmother told me that and she's never wrong about these things."

"Then I confess, my lord, that I'm baffled."

The marquis had smiled at Edington who was reminded, somewhat uncomfortably, of a tiger about to consume its prey.

"I'm not." Harworth's response had been chilling in its quality. "She's got some sort of hold over Stratton and I'm going to find out what it is."

By the time his lordship reached Brindle Mill, news had come of the death of Jeremy Worsley. It was Mabel who greeted the marquis, overcome by the presence of so grand a personage, stuttering and turning red as she tried to explain things to her visitor.

The marquis soon put her at her ease, for it was only his equals whom he reduced to tatters when they exasperated him. He listened to all that Mabel had to say, vastly relieved to learn that his son was safe and Ruby apparently no worse for her experience.

"Where are they now?" he enquired when Mabel finally ran out of steam. "Are they at the earl's house or Miss Travers' cottage?"

"Neither, sir. Message said they were staying on for a while with the squire and his wife. Didn't think he liked Miss Ruby very much, but it seems from what I've heard that he's real broken up about Mr. Jeremy, and she was with him at the last. 'Spect she'll be going home later on."

"Then I shall allow myself the pleasure of calling upon her. Meanwhile, there is someone else whom I have to see. You have been most helpful, Miss Birtwhistle. I am much in your debt."

He kissed Mabel's hand with great panache, leaving her most flustered than ever. Then he ordered Plesshey, his coachman, to take him to Raygreen.

Annora's butler opened the door, taken aback by the arrival of such an unexpected caller. His experienced eye ran over the marquis's apparel, which a prince could have worn without shame. In the drive beyond was an equipage which must have cost a small fortune.

"Who shall I say is calling, sir?"

"You will not announce me."

The butler opened his mouth to protest at such extraordinary behaviour when he found his eyes locked with Harworth's.

"Go back to your pantry and take this for your trouble. Which room is Lady Annora in?"

"The drawing-room, there on the left, but she won't like it."

"You're right; she won't."

The marquis's rejoinder sent a shiver down the servant's spine and when Harworth waved him away he was really quite glad to go.

Annora rose from her chair as Harworth sketched a bow. He was the last person she had expected to see, for it had never occurred to her that he would interest himself in some obscure cotton mill. She imagined he had washed his hands of Stratton's project long ago. It was also a trifle unnerving to find the marquis cognisant of the fact that she, too, was in Lancashire. They were not close acquaintances and she couldn't begin to think who had told him where she was.

She was about to enquire the reason for his visit when he said softly:

"There are one or two questions I have to ask you, madam, and please remember that when you begin to lie I shall know it." The thin lips hardened to an even more forbidding line. "You have used up eight of your lives already; I counsel you not to waste the ninth. If Stratton or Miss Travers had been hurt, you wouldn't have had a ninth life to put into hazard. I should have seen to that."

Annora felt a sudden spasm of nervousness. The marquis's gaze was decidedly inimical and, from his opening remarks, it was clear that his lordship must have been told something of what had been going on. She tried to put a bold face on it for, after all, Harworth was only a man and she'd always been able to handle the opposite sex with consummate ease.

"My lord, I have no idea what you mean ..."

He silenced her with a brief motion of his hand.

"Let me save us both a great deal of time. Since my son became the owner of Brindle Mill the place has been carefully watched. So, madam, have you, and your lover, Lionel Whitcombe. There is very little I don't know, for my agents are experts in this sort of thing, and your maid drinks too much and talks too loudly. However, there are a few points to clear up, such as why Sebastian has asked you to marry him. I shall also want confirmation from you as to what you and Whitcombe did which has caused lives to be lost. Now, my first question is ..."

Annora was still shaking when the marquis rose to go. She had never lived through such a dreadful half hour in her whole existence, nor had she realised that any man could be as deadly as Martin Clare was. She had always been supremely confident in dealing with the foolish creatures; now she had met her match and had no weapons with which to fight him.

She hadn't intended to tell him a thing. She was well aware that a confession would expose her to the due processes of law. It was also obvious after the first five minutes that the marquis would have no compunction in dragging her off to face justice. But she couldn't withstand him, and he already knew so much. Somehow she found herself blurting out everything for, as he told her silkily, it was her one and only chance of saving her skin.

At the door, Harworth turned to looked back at her.

"I have some advice for you," he said and his tone sent a fresh quiver through her. "I think you should go to Europe for a holiday. Shall we say for about five years? I'm sure you understand now what I would do should you fail to heed my suggestion."

She nodded dumbly, thankful he was on his way out. She understood only too well what Clare was talking about. She had planned a death and the scheme had failed. If Harworth decided to do the same thing there was no doubt that his plan would work.

"Go before the end of the week. I'm not a patient man. I'm also going to see your fellow-conspirator. I think I'll be able to convince him that a trip to the West Indies to inspect his properties there would be a wise move."

At first, Lionel Whitcombe blustered and swore a great deal, but that was because, like Lady Eyre, he had misread the Marquis of Harworth's mettle. But he put great store by his own hide and it didn't take him long to realise the danger he was in, nor the utter ruthlessness of Martin Clare. When his lordship raised the question of Cuddy Dalton, Whitcombe began to crack. The marquis's knowledge was so detailed he could have been listening in to every conversation which he, Whitcombe, had had with Annora, Rowney, and others in his pay. He wasn't the only one who had paid men to talk; the marquis had done the same and to greater effect.

The marquis, satisfied that Dalton was innocent, pounced for the last time.

"You're luckier than you deserve, Whitcombe. If you'd succeeded in what you were trying to do to Stratton, you wouldn't be here now. I suppose I should seek proof of your part in the deaths of those unfortunates you used like pawns, but that would take time and I don't want my name dragged into a sordid mess like this. However, if you stay in England I shall be forced to change my mind. Take ship, whilst there's still time, or you'll end your days in Newgate or on the scaffold."

"Very satisfactory," said Harworth to Plesshey as he took his seat in the coach again. "Now that that tiresome business is out of the way, I think I'll pay my respects to Miss Travers. I've had enough of unpleasant people for one day."

* * *

When Sebastian finally returned to the cottage with Ruby he found to his consternation that his father had suddenly appeared out of the blue. He was ensconced in the only comfortable chair, having eaten rather well, and been further fortified by brandy from Wallis's secret hoard.

Not a word had been spoken by Ruby or Sebastian on their journey from Coombridge Manor. They had so much to say, but neither could find the courage to break the oppressive silence.

Martin Clare studied his son's face and then looked at his companion. She was even lovelier than reports had led him to believe, but her sadness was like a yoke round her shoulders.

After a somewhat stilted introduction by the earl, Harworth said lightly:

"You don't have to worry about Whitcombe and Annora Eyre any more. They're going abroad for reasons of health."

"You've seen them?" Sebastian had been contemplating the floor, not at all sure what his father was going to make of Ruby. "Both of them?"

"Of course. Why else would they be fleeing the country? I take it that this intelligence has done nothing to lighten your burdens, whatever they are?"

"No, my lord." Sebastian wasn't really surprised to hear that his august parent had got to work so swiftly. If he had learned anything in his twenty-five years it was that the marquis was capable of almost anything. "I don't give a damn about them. I only care about ..."

As his voice trailed away, the marquis gave a faint smile.

"Yes, I've been kept well-informed about this enterprising young woman."

"Oh?" Stratton's brows met sharply. "How is that?"

Harworth explained briefly and succinctly and Sebastian said tightly:

"You set spies on me?"

"Don't be ridiculous. Did you really think I'd turn you

away for a year without knowing what you were up to? My spies, as you call them, told me all about the problems at the mill, Whitcombe, and Annora Eyre, but the most important enquiries, about Miss Travers, I dealt with myself. Your grandmother insisted I should make those my personal business and she was right. You're lucky that Ruby returns your feelings."

Sebastian's fleeting indignation had faded. In a way it was rather reassuring to know that his apparently indifferent sire cared enough to watch over him, but he had to put the marquis right on one point.

"I'm afraid she doesn't, not any more. You see, I behaved quite unpardonably. I said and did things which no woman could ever forgive."

Harworth, who was watching Ruby's eyes, seeing the love and longing in them, sighed.

"Really, you're a complete cretin. I thought you had enough knowledge of women to know whether one of them loved you or not." He abandoned his offspring as a hopeless case and turned to Ruby instead. "Well, my dear, since you appear to have more sense in your little finger than Stratton has in his whole body, tell me how do you feel about him, whatever he's said or done."

Sebastian had mentioned his father once or twice, although not the fact that he was a marquis. Ruby had formed the opinion that he must be nothing short of an ogre and someone to avoid at all cost. She had never expected to meet him, but now that she had she rather liked what she saw. It was clear that he was a man who came straight to the point, as she herself was wont to do. She hadn't got time for foolish pretence and polite lies, and she was sure Harworth hadn't either.

"I love him quite terribly. I know he thinks I'm immoral, but …"

"No, I don't." Sebastian interrupted her quickly, half-raising his hand as if to take hers. "I know the truth about that now. Annora found out about us, so she sent that man to rape you. She wanted to punish you and thought that would be the way to cause you the most pain."

"And she planned the attempt on your life." The marquis intervened, seeing his son's distress. "For some time Annora has wanted to be Sebastian's wife. He had fobbed her off by saying he'd consider it if the mill failed. She became Whitcombe's mistress in exchange for his services in bringing about the destruction of the factory. When it dawned on Stratton, somewhat belatedly, that this was what was behind all the trouble, he told her that if she would leave you alone, and see what the workers were no longer at risk, he would marry her.

"She agreed, although she'd no intention of letting you live because she knew how Sebastian felt about you. When she told Whitcombe to call off his men, he refused because he was determined to do away with you. She promised to see that you were dealt with in some other way, which would look like an accident. Whitcombe agreed to that. If he hadn't, she told him he wouldn't get into her bed again. He is so besotted by her that she could do anything with him.

"Lady Eyre made a full admission of all this when I saw her to-day. I was able to make her see the folly of trying to hide anything from me."

Ruby was staring at the earl.

"You would have done that for me?" she asked faintly. "You would have married her to save me, and the others of course?"

"I would have married her a hundred times to save you alone."

She blushed, but Stratton was bent on self-abasement.

"None of this makes any difference. When I saw the man with you I believed you unchaste. I made judgments, when I should have trusted you. You'll never forget that. How could you?"

"Why don't you let her make up her own mind?" The marquis was trying to conceal his amusement. He had forgotten how intense love could be when one was young.

"Madam, can you bring yourself to overlook what Stratton did?"

"Yes, of course. His mistake was quite understandable."

"What I did afterwards wasn't."

The marquis raised his eybrows.

"Dear me, what an exciting time the pair of you must have had."

The earl glared at his father and was promptly put in his place.

"Don't look at me like that. You brought all this on yourself. Now, Ruby, you say you love my son."

"Oh, I do, but you'd never let me marry him and I won't be his, or any other man's, mistress. At one time I thought I could give myself to him completely but I changed my mind."

"I should hope so," returned Harworth severely. "As to what I will or will not allow, permit me to be the judge of that. I've had quite a change of heart on that score since I first heard about you."

"Perhaps, but I come from plain stock." Ruby wasn't apologising simply stating a fact. "My blood isn't good enough for your family, my lord."

"I was told by a very wise old lady that it wouldn't be the end of the world if just for once a Clare failed to marry a duchess. Besides, your blood's not that bad."

"You've been misinformed." Ruby was anxious to set the record straight. "My mother's people were quite humble."

"But your father's weren't. Didn't you realise that you were Warren Askwith's daughter?"

Ruby was vaguely aware that Sebastian had given a slight exclamation, but then he melted away with everything else as she began to remember things. There was Vinnie's unusual anger when Elsie had spoken of the portrait of Lady Helen; her mother's refusal to let her keep the red dress, which she must have seen as a sign that Askwith wanted to acknowledge his daughter. Sir Warren's gentleness with Vinnie had always been something more than courtesy, although she'd put it down to the fact that he had a kind heart and perfect manners. It was why he had scrawled a brief note of apology, and why he had left Waterfields to her. She said slowly:

"I had no idea. How did you find out? Are you sure it's true?"

She knew it had to be. A man such as Harworth would always ensure that his information was accurate, but she wanted evidence to cling to.

"I'm very sure. When my agents told me about you, they also mentioned the staff who'd worked at Waterfields since you arrived there. They spoke of a certain Mrs. Boddy. As she'd been Askwith's nurse, I guessed she would know all his secrets. I went to see her."

"Your agents were indeed busy, my lord."

The marquis flicked a warning glance at the earl.

"This is Ruby's business, Stratton, be quiet."

Ruby was still trying to come to terms with the startling announcement, but she knew there was more to come.

"Yes it is my business. Will you please explain things to me, for I'm totally bewildered?"

"Yes, of course." Harworth nodded. "I'll tell you everything, for it's right that you should know. Mrs. Boddy didn't want to talk to me, but I persuaded her that unless she did, you might lead the same sad and empty life which your parents endured. One of my men was quick enough to pick up the fact that the relationship between your mother and her employer was unusual. I wanted to know why. Fortunately, Mrs. Boddy is a woman of some sense and could see how important the matter was."

He paused, but Ruby was impatient.

"Please go on; don't stop now."

"Well, it seems that about eighteen months before you were born, Warren Askwith went to stay with a favourite aunt just outside Manchester. He often did so becuse he didn't get on well with his father and elder brother. As you may have heard, his mother died at his birth.

"Your mother was a maid in his aunt's house and after a while they became lovers. It wasn't a casual *affaire*. It was a strong, enduring passion. Then his father and brother were killed in a coaching accident. When he went to say good-bye to your mother he found she had been dismissed because she was pregnant. Askwith discovered from another servant where she had gone and followed her.

"He begged her to marry him, but she refused because she cared for him too much to ruin his life. In his eyes, he was to good to marry a servant, and it's true that his family was a very old one and of great distinction. He wept, it seems, but she stood firm. That was the measure of her devotion.

"He left her money and made her promise that when you were born she would go to Waterfields as his housekeeper. He, too, loved deeply and couldn't face life without her. His plan was the only alternative to marriage. He said his staff wouldn't question her arrival. He would tell them his aunt had recommended Vinnie for the post.

"For once in his life Warren was insistent and Vinnie gave in but, I suspect, reluctantly. I think she had foreseen what was going to happen. Nevertheless, she agreed and in due course travelled to Waterfields with you.

"When she saw the place she was overawed by it and it made her see more clearly than ever how far apart their worlds really were. From that moment onwards she refused to continue their relationship, although she worshipped Askwith and knew he returned her feelings. Suddenly it seemed to her furtive and dirty, especially now that she had a child to rear; Warren's child."

The marquis looked at Ruby's wide eyes and felt a twinge of envy. He really couldn't see what Stratton had done to deserve so delightful a creature.

"Your father wanted to call you Robina," he went on, "but your mother said it was too fanciful for the likes of you. So just remember that, young woman."

Ruby gave him a smile which made him feel quite weak. It

was obvious that if he hadn't been prepared to consent to her marriage with Sebastian, the latter would have run away with her and no one could have blamed him if he had.

"Also," the amusement was gone, "she was worried because her brother knew the truth. She was always afraid that he would betray her and, more importantly, Askwith. That was why she wouldn't stand up to Cuddy Dalton as everyone thought she should. To put your mind at rest, m'dear, he didn't kill anyone. Rowney murdered the man in question and placed the blame on your uncle. It was a lever to force you to sell Waterfields to his master. But to go back to your father. He was grief-stricken, but he accepted your mother's decision and they went on loving one another although they never shared a bed again."

"How did Mrs. Boddy know all this?" Ruby felt a constriction in her throat. She was recalling the time when she had seen Vinnie and Askwith together on the upper landing, sensing something strange about their quietness. They hadn't been talking about menus; they were just making do with what they had of each other. If Vinnie had loved Warren just a fraction of the way she herself loved Sebastian, life must have been a kind of hell for her. "Did mother tell her?"

"Yes, but she wasn't gossiping. She became ill with a fever and lay for several days and nights in a delirium. The whole tale came out then, bit by bit as she re-lived it. She called for Warren by name and said: 'Try to understand, my love, try to understand.'

"When she was better, Mrs. Boddy told her quite frankly what had occurred. It appears that Vinnie broke down for what was probably the first and last time in her life, and confessed her assumed name and her fear about her brother giving her away. Mrs. Boddy gave her word not to repeat the confidence and she wouldn't have done unless I'd explained about you and Sebastian. As Warren and Vinnie were both dead, and you and my son are young with all your years in front of you, Mrs. Boddy did what she thought your mother and father would have wanted her to do. She told me the truth."

Ruby said shakily:

"It's a dreadfully sad story, isn't it?"

"Painfully so." The marquis was very gentle. "Your mother was a brave woman."

"Yes she was. So was my father in his way, wasn't he?"

"Indeed, but don't you think one tragic love story is enough for any family?"

"I suppose so, but I'm a bastard, my lord. I'm still not good enough for Sebastian."

The marquis gave her a very straight look.

"If I say you are, you are. If you're going to be my daughter-in-law the first lesson you'll have to learn is not to argue with me. By the way, Mrs. Boddy sent you her warmest greetings. It seems she was very fond of you."

"As I was of her. We all cried the day she left. She grew too old to work and Sir Warren ... that is ... my father ... couldn't afford her any more."

"Quite. Now, Stratton, let's deal with you. Do you want Ruby to be your wife or not?"

"More than anything else in the world." Sebastian turned to look at Ruby and saw her eyes fill with tears. "She is my life; without her there is nothing for me."

"Well, if I were you I should do something about it," said Harworth and moved unhurriedly to the door. "At least I shall know you won't be allowed to drink too much, gamble for high stakes, or ... well ... not that either. By the way, the pair of you are to come home."

"I don't think I want to." Sebastian was feeling decidedly light-headed. "I'm going to stay here and build another mill where men and women are treated like human beings and children will not be allowed to enter its gates."

Harworth was dry.

"Yes, your grandmother warned me you'd say that. I'll compromise in that case. You may stay until my first grandchild is on his or her way; then you'll return to

London. Is that understood?"

"Yes, my lord." Sebastian wasn't really listening. He had other things on his mind. "That is, if Ruby really wants me after what I did."

"For God's sake kiss the poor, wretched girl and put her out of her misery," said Harworth in exasperation. "Can't you see even now what she feels for you?"

"I'll explain it to him, my lord."

Ruby and the marquis exchanged a rather special smile.

"It looks as though you'll have to. I'll say one thing in Stratton's favour, even if he is a numskull. He always did have impeccable taste when it came to picking a filly. I'm glad to see he hasn't lost his touch. You'll do very well, m'dear. Yes, very well indeed."

* * *

Fifteen blissful minutes later, Sebastian said quietly:

"If I could collect together all the love in the world I would give it to you along with my dreams, which are all about you."

Ruby held one of his hands between hers, filled with wonderment. She had to keep assuring herself that what had happened was really true, and that she wasn't going to wake up suddenly and find that Sebastian had gone.

"You can't do that." She touched his cheek with her lips. "You see, I've just been to market and bought most of the love there was to be had. I was going to give it to you."

Sebastian was conscious of a great sense of peace and contentment. Ruby was going to be his cherish for all their days. She would brighten his waking hours with her radiance and at night he would fall asleep in her arms when passion was temporarily spent.

"Why don't we put our love together in one large basket and share it equally?" he asked, marvelling anew at what the closeness of her body could do to him. "Would you like that?"

"Very much, and each day we could dip into it and take out kisses and caresses as we pleased."

"And later, when everyone has gone to bed, we could help ourselves to something even more enjoyable."

She laughed, never one to put on false and maidenly blushes.

"I'd like that better still. I wish we were married already. I want to be yours now, this very minute."

"You're shameless, but how lucky I am that you are. I think I'll have another token from you on account."

As she held up her face for his kiss she paused, momentarily anxious.

"Sebastian, you won't ever stop caring, will you?"

His smile reassured her, his words laying her fears to rest for good.

"Not in this world or the next. I'll go on caring for you until time runs out. Oh, Ruby, my dear sweet weaver of spells, I wonder if you know how much I love you."

Their kiss lasted a long while; then Stratton gave her a gentle shake.

"Enough of that, you seductive baggage, or I shall forget where I am. Besides, we've got work to do. Come with me if you please, Miss Travers. You and I have got a factory to build."